D1151118

*Trees*

*in the*

*Pavement*

# Trees in the Pavement

Jennifer Anne Grosser

**CF4·K**

Copyright © 2008 Jennifer Anne Grosser
ISBN 978-184550-342-0

Christian Focus Publications
Geanies House, Fearn, Tain, Ross-shire, IV20 1TW,
Scotland, United Kingdom
www.christianfocus.com
e-mail: info@christianfocus.com

Cover design by Daniel van Straaten
Printed and bound in Denmark
by Nørhaven Paperback A/S

All rights reserved. No part of this publication may be reproduced, stored
in a retrieval system, or transmitted, in any form, by any means, electronic,
mechanical, photocopying, recording or otherwise without the prior
permission of the publisher or a licence permitting restricted copying. In
the U.K. such licences are issued by the Copyright Licensing Agency, Saffron
House, 6-10 Kirby Street, London, EC1 8TS. www.cla.co.uk

*For Liridona, who isn't Zari, but might have
understood her in the circumstances.*

# Contents

# Changes

*T*hey were cutting the branches off the trees again. When Zari first arrived in East London, she had wondered about the trees. She had never seen any fields and farms in London, like there were at home in Kosovo. But there were more trees. Or at least you noticed them here. In Kosovo, there were entire forests, but no one thought about them because they were just there. In London, the trees looked uncomfortable growing out of the pavement, as if they were refugees in a foreign country, too, maybe, with their branches sawn off so they wouldn't bother anyone. They bothered Zari. They grew great green leaves from their stubby branches anyway, which shaded her in summer and sat in slippery brown piles on the pavement in autumn, but she thought the trees must be unhappy, unable to stretch beyond the terraced houses which hemmed them in.

Zari stretched since they couldn't. Apart from the amputated trees, it was a lovely day, and warm for February. It was too early for leaves, so she could especially notice the blueness of the sky. If she tilted her head way back and squinted, nearly the only thing she could see was blue. Even the peaked roof of the school disappeared. Zari imagined she was lying in a field at the farm where her grandparents lived in Kosovo, and that there was nothing around her but grass. Her eyelashes, which were thick and got rather in the way, could be the grass.

"Zarifeh!"

Zari's head snapped forward to its upright position. Her mother was coming through the noisy crowd of school children who were waiting, like Zari, for their parents to come and collect them. Her mother always called her just like that, as if she were angry. She wasn't really. Zari supposed sounding angry in the school yard made her mother feel as if she knew what was going on. The crowded yard, the hordes of children from countries she had never heard of before, the chattering in unknown languages, made her nervous. Well, Zari had been nervous at first, too. But not now...

"Noneh!" she cried, running toward her. "Noneh! Guess what we did in school today?"

Her mother wasn't listening as she grabbed Zari's arm and gently pulled her to the part of the school yard where the older children were waiting. Ekrem saw them first. He was the younger of Zari's two brothers, but he was enough older than she that he sometimes acted as if he thought she were still in the Infants' School. Sometimes. Sometimes he was her hero. Today was one of the hero-times. Today she didn't mind when he got to tell his story before hers.

"Guess what happened in school, Noneh?" he asked in nonchalant Albanian through a slightly swollen lip as they headed home.

"Oh yes, *guess* what happened!" Zari chimed in. "A Paki tried to steal my lunch!" She glanced around quickly to make sure none of the South Asian children walking home with their mothers had heard her rude name for them. None of them seemed to have, or else they didn't recognize it when it was surrounded by Albanian.

"He did steal it," put in Ekrem dryly. "But I caught him, didn't I?"

Zari laughed. "Noneh, he came huffing over like this." She stomped along the pavement for a few steps, snorting through her nostrils. Ekrem had been so angry she could have sworn she saw little puffs of smoke coming out of his nose, like the old bull on grandfather's farm. "And then he said, 'You...'" Ekrem suddenly wrapped an arm around her stomach and clapped a hand over her mouth.

"I *said*," he cleared his throat dramatically, "'Hand over my sister's lunch and clear off!' Well, he wouldn't."

9

"He said, 'Why should I?'" put in Zari, freeing herself from her brother's clutches.

"So then I said it a little louder: 'Hand over my sister's lunch and clear off!'"

"'Or else!'" added Zari.

"Or else," agreed Ekrem. "So I gave him 'or else'." He crossed his arms smugly over his chest as his mother unlocked the door of their house.

Most of the houses in East London were tall and thin and all stuck together, without any more room to stretch than the trees had. The roofs were of red pottery or black slate shingles mostly; they were the only part of the houses Zari liked. Her family's house in East London, which really belonged to East London and not to her family at all, was the kind with red shingles.

Zari remembered the houses in Kosovo were big and wide and short. She thought they sprawled over the land comfortably and lazily, maybe kind of like American houses but not quite. She knew what American houses looked like even though she had never been to America, because she had seen them on television. She couldn't remember Kosovar roofs; they might have been made of straw, or she might have been thinking of something she saw in a book at school.

She never admitted it to her brothers, but her own memory of Kosovo wasn't really very good. She hadn't even been old enough for the Infants' School when she arrived in London with her mother and brothers and unmarried sister. But her mother remembered everything—even how many chickens grandmother had had. So Zari memorized her mother's memories and talked about them as if she knew. The rest of it she did know. She couldn't exactly picture the farm, or the house where they had lived before they came to England. But she remembered when everything changed.

They were still in Kosovo then, and the change began with a phone call from her father. In the time when she could still see and know the farm and the house, she had no real memory of her father. He had gone to England when she was only two. They said it was to make money for the family and send it back to them, but she was sure there was some other reason they weren't telling her as well. He had had a job in Kosovo, hadn't he?

In any case, he had been in England for most of Zari's life, and phone calls to Kosovo were expensive for him, so it was always an occasion when he made one. The boys, who couldn't go to school since the Albanian ones had been shut down, would dash in from whatever trouble they had been getting into and tear the receiver out of their mother's hands, quarrelling good-naturedly over who would get to speak first. Jasmina, their older sister, would sit in the corner waiting her turn patiently, with a silent smile on her face.

Zari never wanted to speak to her father. He seemed loud to her. Maybe like her oldest brother Agron. But she knew Agron, and she didn't know this boisterous voice in the telephone. "How's my Zarifeh?" he would bellow after her timid hello.

"Fine," she would say. Sometimes it was hardly more than a whisper.

"Are you taking good care of your mother?"

"Yes."

"Are you staying away from the cows?" She had had an accident with her grandfather's bull, the one that blew smoke from its nostrils. She still limped because of it.

"Yes."

"Have you got anything to tell your old Boba?"

"No."

"Give the phone to your mother then."

Zari was not sure if her mother wanted to talk to her father either. Whenever the phone rang, Noneh turned white, and smiles and frowns would flit across her face faster than clouds across a day that couldn't decide whether it wanted to be sunny or stormy. She would grip the receiver with knuckles as white as her face, and talk in single syllables like Zari until she got used to it.

From what the children could hear, the conversation was nearly always the same. First Boba would ask about the family—not just his children, but Noneh's parents, and his parents, and their brothers and sisters. Noneh loved talking about family, and by the time that part of the phone call was over, she was a bit more relaxed. Then they would talk about money: Boba had found a job. Boba had lost his job. Boba had got a better job and would be sending them some more money this month. He hoped it would get there. Noneh always repeated everything he said when they were talking about money, so the children would know. Zari knew the money part was over when her mother got very quiet all of a sudden and then giggled. The giggle always sounded nervous and relieved at the same time.

When it came, Jasmina would say, "Let's see what Grandmother's up to," even if Grandmother was only in the next room. Or, "Shall we go say hello to the chickens?" Or, "How about coming to Gona's with me? She'll be happy to hear about Boba's new job." Antigona was their oldest sister, who was married and had a little girl of her own. Then Jasmina would take Zari's hand and lead her out of the room, so Zari never got to find out what the last part of the phone call was about.

"Doesn't Noneh like to talk to Boba?" Zari asked Jasmina once.

"Of course she does! It's just the telephone makes her nervous. You know how Noneh is about machines."

Zari knew. But even the telephone? Well, maybe. Maybe that was why Zari didn't like talking to Boba either. Maybe it would be different when she actually saw him.

One day there was a phone call, but when Agron wrenched the phone out of his mother's hands, he immediately gave it back. "Boba says he can't talk to me now," he said, puzzled. Noneh shooed them all out of the house, and then she talked on that telephone for a long time.

When Zari came back in later, having gone to visit Antigona and the baby by herself, the house was in quiet uproar. "Hush!" her mother hissed, pulling her through the door and closing it quickly behind her.

"What--?" Zari asked.

"Zarifeh, precious, you mustn't talk loudly—the police will hear us."

There had been trouble with Serbian police in the past, but it was before Zari could remember. She knew about it only because of her brothers' talk—maybe it was even before she was born. Sometimes they heard of an "outbreak" of the Serbs against the Albanians in another village. Sometimes even families close by still had trouble with the police. But her family hadn't had any in ages, except for once when a couple of officers decided it would be fun to steal some chickens. One of the Serbs was even friendly to Zari. He knew her name and gave her sweets when her mother wasn't around and his friends weren't either. Her mother would not have approved.

"So what if they hear us?" Zari asked. "Are we being bad?"

"No!" Her mother, who was cramming too many things into a very small box, sat back on her heels and looked indignant. "The Serbs are the ones—never mind.

14

We're going away, lovely. We're going to visit Boba."

This was a new thought. For as far back as Zari could remember, her mother and sisters and brothers had talked about "going to visit Boba." "When we go to visit Boba," they said, again and again and again. But no one had ever actually gone to visit him, and Zari supposed they never would. Where was it he lived? England? Was it very far away?

It was ages away. The day after the phone call, Noneh spent the whole of it looking as she did at the beginning of a telephone conversation with Boba. That afternoon, Uncle Mufail came with his little white car, and the family packed a few small boxes into the back of it and crammed themselves into it, too: Mufail, Noneh, Zari, Ekrem, Agron, and Jasmina. Antigona and the grandparents had to stay behind. The grandparents were too old, and Antigona was married and had her own family. Noneh waited until the car left the village before she started crying. Then she really cried—sobbed and sobbed. She had not been able to say goodbye to her oldest child. Not a proper goodbye, anyhow. Late the evening before, she had taken Zari with her and they said hushed goodbyes at Antigona's house. Noneh and Antigona had cried then, too, but it had to be quiet and brief. If any of the police on the lookout had heard any of it, they would have known the family leaving their village in a little white car was not, as they claimed, going on a picnic with their uncle in the mountains.

# A Lorry Full of Cheese

*N*oneh had a look at Ekrem's swollen lip without comment when they got inside their council house. Then he and Zari raced up the narrow stairs to see who could throw whose school satchel on the bed first. Zari's had a library book, some pencils, and a notebook inside. She had some homework she was meant to do, but it was only a little bit, and it was maths, which was easy. It could wait until later. In the meantime, she had noticed that her mother's friend, Anita, was there, sitting on one of the settees they had got from friends in Central London. Anita lived in a nearby neighbourhood and had a little boy who was, Noneh said, the same age as Antigona's little girl. Zari loved him, but only for about half an hour. After that she got bored. Ahmed couldn't talk very much, in either

17

English or Albanian, and he didn't remember anything about Kosovo.

The television was on as usual when they came in, showing one of the Australian soap operas. But Anita didn't seem to be watching it. Noneh sent Zari into the kitchen to refill the glass of soft drink her guest had drunk while Noneh was picking the children up from school. When Zari came back, the women were talking about the family they had left behind in Kosovo. They had this conversation whenever Anita came over, which was often. "I haven't heard from Antigona this week," her mother was saying. "It worries me. The phone lines are cut off again. Or maybe they had to go to the mountains, she and her man. And then what is for them?"

"You should be proud if your son-in-law will fight," Anita said. "My brother!" Anita was unhappy with her brother. Zari knew she thought he was weak because he wouldn't join the Albanians in their liberation army. Zari wondered if he was. In that case, her brothers weren't weak—neither of them. Agron would come home from secondary school and read the month-old Albanian paper that friends in Central London gave them, and he would growl. "If I could get my hands on one of those Serbs, they'd wish they'd never seen an Albanian!"

"Don't they already wish that?" Zari had asked once, but Agron had growled at her, too, as if she were a Serb, and told her she was stupid. Zari never asked again.

"What did you bring us here for, Boba?" Agron

demanded one evening. "To sit and read old news about our families dying, when I could join the KLA and fight those...?"

Noneh covered Zari's ears so she couldn't hear what Agron said about those Serbs, but Zari had a pretty good idea. Noneh wouldn't be happy if she knew what the words meant that Ekrem had been learning in English lately. The words he used to that Pakistani boy at lunch today. Ekrem was as unfriendly as Agron when it came to the Serbs, but, lacking any Serbs to fight in the school yard, he took out his frustration on Pakistanis, mostly. Zari didn't like Pakistanis either. They took her lunch, for example. Well, one of them took her lunch. Once.

Zari's brothers were brave. They would fight if they were in Kosovo, and they would fight here, and Agron said when he was old enough, he would go back to Kosovo and join the KLA in spite of his father. Ekrem said, "Me, too!" Boba, who was normally as boisterous in real life as he was on the telephone, would always get quiet when Agron talked like that. Noneh would murmur, "Pray the war doesn't last so long."

"It will last," said Agron. "They will always be fighting. I'm glad—I want my chance!"

"Listen to yourself!" Boba snapped.

Zari was listening to both of them. Was Boba weak like Anita's brother? She didn't want him to be; she loved her father now that she knew him. He laughed and teased and played with her and Ekrem when he was home. But he would not fight. He seemed to hate the Serbs as much as anyone she knew. But he had not stayed in Kosovo; he had even left it before his family did, and then, instead of coming back to them, he had sent money so they could come to him. It had turned out to be much more than a visit.

The night they left the village in the little white car, Uncle Mufail took Noneh, Agron, Ekrem, Jasmina, and Zari to his own house. Mufail's wife, Aunt Doruntina, was ready for them with a big meal; it was like a party. There was a big bowl of chicken in its juice with a hint of tomatoes, and a giant loaf of bread from which to wrench bits to sop up that juice, and a great jar of pickled green tomatoes, and one of pickled peppers, and one of hot chillies, and a plate of feta cheese. The best part for Zari was the enormous pan of *pide*: layers and layers of buttery, eggy, dough, baked in the oven especially for someone to dig their fingers into and pull out long strips. The children did just that, with the pide and the chicken and everything else as well, juice dripping down to their elbows in their enthusiasm. Jasmina was a little more dignified in her eating, but her eyes shone as she saw the feast. It was a strange gleam, Zari noticed—not like the one in her brothers' eyes. It was as if Jasmina thought this was the last meal she would ever see.

Noneh hardly ate anything. "Eat!" Doruntina urged her. "You need strength for the journey."

"Where did you get all this food?" Noneh asked. "You

have made three meals here instead of one. We will eat you into poverty."

"You are family," said Doruntina. "And this is an occasion. You deserve such a feast." Doruntina's mouth said the occasion was a holiday to England. Her eyes said they might never meet again. Noneh and Mufail were brother and sister, but Noneh and Doruntina had not always seen eye to eye on things. Grandmother said, "If we had but known what that Isuf's daughter would get up to, we would never have agreed to their marriage!" As if it had not been Grandmother herself who had arranged the marriage in the first place. But now, with Doruntina's words, Noneh burst into tears and the two women held each other as if they were really sisters, or at least best friends.

Jasmina looked at the piece of pide in her hand guiltily, nibbled at it, and stopped. Suddenly Zari wasn't so hungry either. What was going on? They were only going to visit Boba, weren't they?

The next day, Mufail took them into Prishtina, the capital city. Zari had heard of it, but she had never been there before. She had never been to any city before, she didn't think. It was big and noisy and there were more police even than in the village. The buildings were grey and tall, and some of them had holes as well as windows, but Zari thought the city was beautiful and amazing. She wanted to roll down the car window so she could put her head out and see the tops of the buildings, but her uncle

21

wouldn't let her.

They drove past great shops which sold clothes for people who had money. They had money now, Zari reckoned. Boba kept sending them so much; surely they didn't need all of it for the journey to visit him. "Are we going to buy clothes?" Zari asked. "Are we going to get new things for visiting Boba?"

No one answered her, and soon they were driving down a dark narrow street behind some of the shops. Where were they going, and why? Maybe Mufail knew one of the shop owners, who would let them in the back way and give them clothes cheaper. Were they still behind the clothes shops?

When Mufail parked the car next to a big lorry and opened the door, Zari decided they weren't still behind the clothes shops. The smell was terrible. Clothes wouldn't smell like that. "Wait here," Mufail said, getting out. He tiptoed around, like a detective on television, looking this way and that. Then he disappeared around the other side of the lorry, and they didn't see him for a long time. Just as Noneh began acting nervously, he reappeared, smiling. An enormous man with a bald head was with him. He was smiling, too.

"He's fat," Zari said, as her uncle beckoned them to get out of the car.

"Don't say things like that!" Jasmina hissed at her. "Especially not to him. He's going to take us to England, I think; now be nice."

A Lorry Full of Cheese

Zari was especially nice to him then, even when he told Mufail, "Leave now," but the man never seemed to notice. He was especially nice to Jasmina instead. Jasmina noticed, but not with any pleasure. The big man kept saying the most ridiculous things to her sister that Zari had ever heard, and his accent made them sound even more outrageous. Agron said the man was German. Jasmina blushed and pursed her lips and turned away and said nothing.

"You said to be nice," Zari told her accusingly under her breath. "But you're being rude; you're not answering his questions."

"Sometimes that's nicer," Jasmina muttered, and wouldn't explain what she meant.

Fortunately, they didn't have to see the big man very often. Most of the time, he was driving the lorry, and they were huddled in the back, behind stacks and stacks of boxes. Most of the boxes were bound together in bunches with ropes or enormous sheets of plastic. All of the boxes were filled with tins of things like feta cheese and olives—the sorts of things Zari and her family had eaten at Doruntina and Mufail's, as it happened. Only this time they couldn't eat any of it. It was pretty dark in there, and even darker behind the boxes at the back of the lorry. There was just enough room for them all to fit, and if they sat down, no one's heads showed over the stacks.

The ride was blurry in Zari's mind. All she knew

23

was that it seemed like forever, and she was cold, even though Noneh unpacked one of their own boxes and wrapped everyone up in blankets, and they all huddled together. And she was hungry, all the more because of the lorry being full of food that they couldn't eat. And she needed the toilet.

That was when she found out why Uncle Mufail had given them a bucket. "What if it tips over?" Ekrem had asked after Zari had used it. Agron stood up and hung it on some sort of hook or nail he discovered sticking out of the side of the truck. Zari thought it would be even worse if it fell off the hook on their heads than if it tipped over on the floor, but Agron said it wouldn't fall. It did start to smell in there after a while, though.

The next time they saw the driver, he was speaking even before he got the back of the lorry open. Somehow, Noneh didn't think he was speaking to them. "Lie down!" she whispered. "Don't make a sound!" Nobody, Zari thought, would be able to see them behind the boxes, but they might be able to hear them. She closed her mouth tight. She wasn't going to say anything.

"Cover the bucket," Agron added quickly. "It stinks. They'll know we're here for sure. And close your eyes." He seemed to know what his mother was thinking, somehow. "That way, if they have torches, the light won't reflect." Jasmina quickly reached the bucket down, just in time, and put one of their own boxes on top of it, and they all lay down behind the rows of boxes.

24

They had scarcely situated themselves when the door flew open. Zari had already lain down obediently, but along with the fact that Agron's feet were in her face, it was frustrating not to be able to see what was happening. She could just make out through her eyelids, however, that Agron had been right about the torches. She heard what sounded like two men stomping into the truck. They were speaking a language that wasn't Albanian, and crashing about among the boxes on the shelves and shining their torches around. One of them stomped all the way to the back where the plastic-wrapped boxes were. He paused. Zari could tell he was shining the torch right at the wall behind them. She squeezed her eyes shut even tighter. After a few minutes that seemed like hours, he and his friend stomped back to the entrance. Zari heard them jump to the ground with two "oofs." She opened her eyes just in time to see the backs of them, one tall man and one short, and the driver closing the doors.

No one else in her family moved until the vehicle began moving again. But when they did, Zari found herself face to knee with Ekrem. He was standing up. "Didn't you lie down?" she asked.

In fact, he hadn't. As it turned out, he had stood up and watched the entire time. He had stayed behind the boxes with his back to the wall, but he laughed and laughed when he told how the one guard almost shone the torch at him. At that point, Agron sat on him, and then Agron and Noneh and Jasmina spent the next hour scolding him for being so stupid and nearly getting them caught and killed.

Zari agreed that he probably had been stupid, but she was secretly a little envious as well. After her family's anger had died down and they were talking of other things, she crept across to Ekrem, who was sulking to himself. "What did you say those two men looked like?" she whispered. Ekrem's eyes lit up, and for a while the ride stopped being so boring, as the two of them sat together, giggling in whispers about the guards who hadn't managed to catch the refugee family in the back of a lorry full of cheese.

The next time they stopped, however, Ekrem got told off as no one in his family could have done it. They seemed to be driving through forest, and the driver, who must not have had a bucket with him like Zari's family had, had pulled over to go to the toilet in the woods. But after that he opened the back of the truck again and came in himself. He had seen Ekrem standing up, even if the two border guards hadn't. Now the man picked him up by the scruff of the neck and held him in front of his big fat face and let him have it. "You think you're clever, don't you, pup?" he bellowed. "You think you're brave? You nearly got your family caught back there, and if you don't care about them, which you should, care about the fact that I could lose my job for you! I could get arrested. And I don't intend to get arrested for you, either. Which means that if you pull any more stunts like that one, I'm turning you all out at the next border, and you can try your luck with the guards there. You won't see me!"

He went on and on, and Zari wished someone in her family would do something, but they all were too embarrassed by Ekrem's behaviour even to try. Finally she walked up to the man herself. "Look here," she said, "we're all being really nice to you even though you're fat and can't even speak Albanian properly, but you aren't being very nice to my brother at all. Put him down!"

Noneh and Jasmina held their breath. Agron and the driver both looked like they wanted to tell her off next, but instead the driver gave Ekrem one more teeth-rattling shake and set him down. "Keep your heads down," he said gruffly as he stomped back out of the truck.

Ekrem thanked her over and over again once they got back in the truck. "You've never done anything like that before, Zarifeh," he said.

Zari thought about that. He was right. She was only four, and had never spoken to a grown-up like that in her life. Maybe once some things started changing, everything did. Maybe she was changing, too.

"You weren't afraid of him at all!" Ekrem was saying. "Of course, I wasn't either, but I couldn't exactly do anything when he had me by my collar... How come you're so afraid to talk to Boba on the phone then?"

Zari thought about that, too. She didn't know. His

question reminded her that they were going to see Boba. She wondered if she would be afraid of him when she saw him. Her stomach knotted up a little bit, though she didn't know why. It was true; she had not been afraid of the lorry driver when she scolded him, but she still didn't like to think of Boba. The idea of him made her nervous. She crawled back to the other wall and curled up beside her mother. She wondered if Noneh would be afraid to talk to Boba when there wasn't a telephone between them. Then she fell asleep.

Once they got into Paris, France, the lorry driver didn't seem to think they needed him any more. He let them out near a train station. There were a lot of people who didn't pay any attention to Zari and her family, and who probably didn't know how to speak Albanian, either. The language they spoke sounded funny. Zari wondered how anyone could understand anybody else.

In a few minutes, a man came up to Noneh and asked her something quietly. He was so quiet, Zari couldn't hear him, but she was fairly certain he had spoken in Albanian. "Who's he?" she whispered to Jasmina.

"He's going to help us get tickets," Jasmina whispered back.

They walked over to a ticket counter and the man spoke to the woman behind the counter. He gave her some money and she gave him tickets—five of them.

"Now wait over here," the man said, leading them away. "In a few minutes I will go somewhere else and get your other tickets."

Zari wondered what the other tickets were for, if they already had five of them. She asked Noneh. "Only to get to England," said Noneh. "It's still a long way. But don't tell anyone we have two sets of tickets, Zari. Or you, Ekrem." She looked a little annoyed that the man had mentioned more tickets where they could all hear him. Zari wondered why no one could know about the other tickets if they had to use them to get to England.

Noneh also told her that if anyone who didn't speak Albanian properly asked if they had passports and visas, she should say yes, her mother had them. If anyone who did speak Albanian asked, she should say no. This confused Zari. "But do we have them, Noneh?" she asked. She didn't know what a passport or a visa was, but they must be important. Noneh wouldn't answer her. Agron and Jasmina were silent on the subject as well, and Ekrem didn't know what a visa was, either, even though he pretended to.

After a while, the man came back. He gave the tickets to Noneh, and she gave him some money. Zari noticed it was a lot of money. She could not believe that tickets would cost so much, but she understood now why they had not bought new clothes for visiting Boba when they had been in Prishtina.

They got on the train a few minutes later. It was a nice train, and Zari had never been on one before. As soon as the conductor went by for the tickets—Noneh only showed him five—Zari and Ekrem got up and took a long walk up and down the train. They were especially interested in the dining car, but they didn't have any money with them. The food didn't look as nice as what Noneh cooked at home, but they thought it would still cost something and they had nothing. Besides, they couldn't speak French. When they went back to their train carriage and sat down again, Noneh gave them some of the food she had packed. Then they went up and down the train quite a few more times before it stopped in a place called Calais. It stopped there for a long time. A lot of people got off the train and a lot of new people got on. When it started again, they had a new conductor. Noneh showed him their other tickets. Nobody asked for a passport or visa.

Zari was getting sleepy, and the train was very warm with all those people. Before she knew it, she had fallen asleep. She slept for a very, very long time.

When she woke up, a man's giant face was looking at her, and she realized that the arms below the face must be holding her. She didn't recognize the face, but just as she had been brave when she told off the lorry driver, now she wasn't afraid either, and she was still silly with sleep, so she just lay in the strange arms and stared.

The voice that came out of the face was familiar. "How's my Zarifeh, then?" it asked.

Where had she heard that before?

"Don't you know your old Boba?"

A Lorry Full of Cheese

Was this Boba? He looked like an old Ekrem—dark curly hair with bits of grey in it, a long face, straight eyebrows, narrow dark eyes.

"Yes," said Zari.

31

# Bigot

*A*fter school these days, Zari usually went across the street and knocked for her friend Sophie. Sophie was English, and she was in Zari's year at school. She was the one who had started calling Zari "Zari," on the first day of school in Reception. Before that, it had always been Zarifeh, but she soon discovered to her frustration that a lot of people in England had trouble pronouncing her name. She liked it when Sophie called her "Zari," though, and now her brothers and father and sometimes even Jasmina called her that, too. Her mother still called her Zarifeh.

Today, Zari didn't have to knock. Sophie was outside already, playing with some children Zari had never seen before. "Zari!" Sophie called, before Zari could duck back indoors. "Come on—we're playing 'Tag'! You're 'It'!"

She dashed away.

"I don't want to be It," Zari pouted, and turned to go back in the house.

"All right then—I'll be It!" Sophie tore across the street, without watching for cars. Instead of dashing into the house and slamming the door on her friend's face as she had meant to do, suddenly Zari found herself racing down the pavement with Sophie at her heels. By the time Sophie had caught her, Zari was laughing.

"All right! I'll be It!" She swivelled around and chased after her. They were lucky not many cars came down their street. Most of them were parked on the side of the road, and made wonderful places to hide behind and dodge around. It didn't matter how many times their mothers scolded them; they hardly ever watched for cars. The other children, two girls and a boy, had scampered away from Zari as she passed them, but she didn't even look in their direction, or try to tag them, even though she could easily have caught the little boy, who was only about four.

"Oi, Zari!" said Sophie, panting after her friend had finally tagged her, "They're playing, too, you know. You didn't think I was out here playing 'Tag' all on my own before you came out, did you?"

"I don't want to play with them," Zari muttered. She rather hoped they didn't hear her, but almost hoped they did, too. They did. The little boy's face fell and the

34

younger girl started to cry. The older girl made her face look like she hadn't heard anything, but she was trying so hard that Zari knew she had.

It reminded Zari of when her family had first arrived in England and no one had wanted to play with them, either. That was when she had been willing to play with anyone and didn't care where they were from. In those days, the only person who would play with them, sometimes, was Muqeem, the boy next door. He was Pakistani, but he was one of the reasons Zari didn't like them any more.

"How can you be Muslims?" Muqeem had asked once. "Your family eats pork. We can smell it when you're cooking it. And your father drinks beer. I've seen the bottles in your rubbish."

"What were you doing in our rubbish then?" Ekrem had asked irritably. "Were you hungry or something?"

"Noneh doesn't eat pork," Zari had said, when Ekrem had translated the conversation for her. After that, she stopped eating pork as well. But it didn't make her like Muqeem any better. His father came out of the house at that point, dressed in white trousers and a long white shirt, with a round white cap on his head. Muqeem was wearing a white cap as well. It was crocheted, and Zari thought it looked nice against his black hair, but she grew to hate the sight of it after a few weeks. Muqeem would play with them at any time except when he wore that cap; then he would start criticizing them for something like not knowing the Qur'an, until his father came out of the house to take him to mosque school. Zari and Ekrem kept knocking for him anyway, because no one else would play with them at all.

Ekrem was learning English fast in those days, because he was put in school the day they moved into their council house. Zari's English was still appalling, however. She wasn't old enough for school yet; she and Noneh stayed indoors all day and chattered to each other in Albanian. Jasmina did that for a while as well, but then someone arranged for her to get into an English class at the local college. She was a good student, they were told. Her English was improving rapidly. Zari and Noneh's English was stuck.

Then it got even more stuck; Ekrem started making friends at school. Before then, even if there were no other children in the neighbourhood who would play with Zari, Ekrem would come home and play with her, often in English. But once he started making friends with the boys in his class, they would play games like cricket on the pavement, or football in the street, and Ekrem's English friend Robert would taunt, "No girls allowed!"

"No girls allowed!" Ekrem would translate happily into Albanian.

"I know what it means!" Zari retorted in Albanian, too. Goodness knows she heard it enough. Plenty of days she would go inside and feel like the little boy's face looked just now when she said she didn't want to play "Tag" with him and his sisters.

But then she had started school, and she had met Sophie, who, it turned out, had only lived over the road from her all the time. Now she was in Year Three and had someone to play with every day, and she and Sophie could shout to the boys in perfect English, "No boys allowed!"

The looks on the three children's faces made Zari feel bad. She almost said so; she almost said she was sorry. But only weak people, like the people who wouldn't fight the Serbs, said sorry. So instead she said again, louder, "I don't want to play with them."

Sophie looked uncomfortable. "Oh come off it, Zari. They've got to play with somebody, and we're the only lot out here right now. Besides, it's just for a laugh—just so you and I don't have to be It all the time."

"They can play together, can't they?" Zari asked coldly. "There are three of them. That's more than there were when Ekrem and I only had to play with each other. Or they can go across the street and knock for Muqeem. They must be the right sort of Muslim for him. They're Pakis after all."

"It's all right," the oldest girl said suddenly and stiffly from behind them. Her face was pale and she looked angry. "We're just going in anyway. Come on then," she said to her brother and sister. They turned and went quietly into the house.

"What did you do that for, you bigot!" Sophie exploded when the door closed behind them. "Bigot" was Sophie's new word; she had learned it from her dad, whom she visited at weekends. He was what some grown-ups called "liberal," and he didn't care which country people came from or what colour they were. Her mother cared, and since Sophie had to live with her most of the time, she knew how to annoy her more than her father. Sophie's dad's way of looking at the world was the most annoying thing her mother knew, and so Sophie started thinking like her dad, too. She called people "bigot," all the time, including her mother, but she had never called Zari that before. "You bigot!" she said again, for good measure. "They just moved in, too!"

Zari felt herself turning red. "So?" she said. She felt worse and worse, and the only thing she knew to do was make the things coming out of her mouth more and more horrible. "They can just move out again. See if I care."

"Some nice kid you are," Sophie shot back at her.

"Some nice kid *you* are!" Zari retorted. "None of my other friends call me 'bigot!'"

"What other friends?" Sophie shouted.

"I have plenty of other friends!" Zari shouted louder.

"Oh really? Well, you can just play with them, then, because *I'm* not your friend any more!" Sophie turned on her heels and went into her house, slamming the door behind her.

Zari stomped back across the street and knocked on the door—but it wasn't her own door. It was Mrs Jamaica's.

Mrs Jamaica was Zari's next door neighbour on the other side from Muqeem. Her real name was Mrs Dix, but Zari and her brothers knew she was Jamaican before they knew her name. They started calling her that among themselves, and the name stuck. She didn't mind. Mrs Jamaica and her husband, whom they called Mr Jamaica, were the first Jamaicans anyone in Zari's family had ever met. They were the first non-Serbian Christians the children and Noneh had ever met as well.

Noneh was a little bit suspicious of them at first; she was suspicious of everyone who was a Christian. People said England was a Christian country. Boba had lived there for two years before the rest of the family arrived, and he didn't seem to have had any trouble with Christians here, so they couldn't be too much like the Serbs. Still, one never knew when something would happen and everything would change. It had happened in Yugoslavia. But Boba said, "There are Christians and there are Christians."

Zari wondered what that meant.

Noneh must have wondered, too, because Boba had to explain. "There are Christians like the Serbs in Kosovo, who hate to have us here, but they would probably hate to have Mr and Mrs Jamaica here, too. Then there are Christians who just don't care either way. And there are

Christians who want to talk about Jesus all the time and want to make sure you know they do want you here, and if you can come up with a good enough story for why you need it, they'll even lend you money."

Zari wasn't sure which of the last two the Jamaicas were. As far as she knew, they had never lent her family any money. But they went to church every week, and Sophie and her mother, who said they were Christians, too, never did. In any case, Zari liked Mrs Jamaica, whether she was a Christian or not. Sometimes she would pop in at Zari's and have a cup of English tea with Noneh, and sometimes Noneh and Zari would go over to her house instead. Sometimes Zari went there by herself, and Mrs Jamaica would let her watch whatever she was doing (which was usually cooking) and talk to her.

Today, Mrs Jamaica had flour up to her elbows when she answered the door, which meant she was baking. "What's wrong, love?" she asked when she saw Zari's face. "You look like you swallowed a mouthful of jerk seasoning and it went down the wrong pipe!"

Zari knew what jerk seasoning was, because she had tried it in some of Mrs Jamaica's cooking once. She wasn't sure which pipe Mrs Jamaica was talking about however, and she wondered how to tell whether or not it was the wrong one.

"Come on in," said Mrs Jamaica. "I was just making ginger cake; when it comes out of the oven you can have some. In the meantime, you can tell me what's making your face look like a cat with a stuck hair-ball."

"Sophie shouted at me," Zari said glumly, taking off her shoes at the door. Mr and Mrs Jamaica didn't take their shoes off inside the door of their house like Zari and her family did, but Zari usually forgot, and Mrs Jamaica didn't mind. "She says she doesn't want to be my friend any more."

Mrs Jamaica led the way to the kitchen at the back of the house and Zari climbed up on her favourite stool, while Mrs Jamaica did the washing up and talked to her. She didn't ask Zari what she had done to make Sophie yell at her. Zari liked that. The teachers at school would have blamed her straightaway. "Some children are like that," Mrs Jamaica sighed instead. "What can have made her say such an unkind thing?"

"I don't know," Zari mumbled, even though she knew very well. She thought about what she had done to make Sophie say a thing like that. She thought about times when she had said things like that herself. There was silence for a minute.

Then Mrs Jamaica said, "Look, darling, I want to help you, but I can't do that very well if I don't know what's happened. You're going to have to tell me a little more."

"I thought maybe you saw it from your window," Zari said. She rather wished that were true. Even if Mrs Jamaica had seen her behaving badly, it would be better than Zari having to admit it herself, which she knew she would have to do, sooner or later.

Mrs Jamaica shook her head, "No, love. I was back here with my cake the whole time."

"Sophie called me a bigot."

Mrs Jamaica slowly turned around from the sink and looked at her. "Do you know what a bigot is?" she asked.

"Yes," Zari hung her head. "At least, I think so."

"What is it?"

"It's someone who only likes people from their own country and nobody else."

"Something like that," agreed Mrs Jamaica. "Was Sophie right?"

Zari said nothing for a minute and then her head shot up. "Yes!" she exclaimed defiantly. "I don't care! I don't like anyone except Albanians—Albanians and you!"

It was serious, but Mrs Jamaica chuckled. "Funny," she said. "I've never been liked by a bigot before. Why do you only like Albanians and me?"

"Because you're good. And they're good. But only you and Albanians. Everyone else is unkind and they all want to hurt us; I thought maybe Sophie was good, but she isn't either."

"Hmm," murmured Mrs Jamaica, more to herself than to anyone else. "I only know one man who's good, and he... Come on, Zari, don't tell me you don't know *anyone* who isn't Albanian who is kind."

"Just you," said Zari. "I already told you. And Mr Jamaica, too, of course." She wasn't really sure about Mr

42

Jamaica, actually; she didn't know him very well, because he went to work every day. But he seemed all right when she saw him, and anyone with someone as nice as Mrs Jamaica for a wife must be a good person, too.

"You might be surprised," said Mrs Jamaica suddenly. "If you knew me better, I don't think you'd find me all that good, either."

"What do you mean?" Zari asked. She already was surprised, and she hadn't even seen Mrs Jamaica do anything bad yet. She wondered what she could have done that was so terrible. Zari tried to think of the worst thing Mrs Jamaica could have done. Maybe she had killed someone. She had pictures of her daughter over the fireplace in her sitting room, but Zari had never seen the daughter. Maybe Mrs Jamaica had killed her daughter. Maybe all this time Zari and her family had been living next door to a murderess. Zari shivered slightly.

But all Mrs Jamaica said was, "Sometimes Mr Jamaica and I have rows, for example."

Was that all? Boba and Noneh had rows all the time, and they must have been worse than the Jamaicas' ones, because Zari had never heard the Jamaicas rowing through the wall or anything. She told Mrs Jamaica so.

"Of course," said Mrs Jamaica. "Even the most quiet people have rows once in a while. But that doesn't mean it's right. You just had a row yourself just now, and it didn't make you very happy, did it?"

"No."

"Well, then. So we all have rows, and rows are bad, so we all must be a little bit bad, right?"

Zari didn't say anything. She knew she was bad sometimes. But she wasn't as bad as Sophie. She didn't go round calling people bigots. And, "Albanians aren't as bad as *some* people."

"As which people?" Mrs Jamaica asked, not as if she were trying to catch Zari in a trap, but as if they were having a perfectly ordinary and friendly conversation.

"As Pakis."

Suddenly Mrs Jamaica's voice got hard and cold. Zari had never heard her sound like that in her life. "Don't ever use that word in my house again," she said.

"Why?" Zari whispered, hushed by the tone in Mrs Jamaica's voice. "Don't you like them, either?" Maybe Mrs Jamaica was secretly a bigot, too. If that were true, it couldn't be such a terrible thing to be.

The coldness passed right out of Mrs Jamaica's voice and she startled Zari with a hearty laugh. "Don't I like them? What do you mean, 'them'? I have Pakistani friends, though there are a few I don't like, either, but it isn't because they're Pakistani. I don't like all Jamaicans, even. Or probably all Albanians, although you lot are the only ones I know right now, and I like you well enough. But if you're going to talk about a race of people, call them by their proper name, and not some racist nickname."

She left Zari thinking about that and went to answer

the door. Ekrem was on the other side of it. Zari could hear him talking in the passage. "Noneh wants to know if you've seen Zari?"

"Zari? You mean that brown-eyed girl with the long wavy hair, lives next door to me?"

Zari giggled from the kitchen.

"Yes, she's here. We're just having a chat. Would you like to join us?"

Zari held her breath. The conversation was uncomfortable enough without Ekrem. She wondered if Mrs Jamaica could get Ekrem to stop saying "Paki." She wondered if Mrs Jamaica would stop being friends with her family if she found out that none of them liked anyone except Albanians.

"My mother says Zari needs to come home now."

"Could she at least stay until she's had a piece of ginger cake? It's just about to come out of the oven, and I promised her a piece. You could have one as well."

Ekrem hesitated.

"Never mind," said Mrs Jamaica. "I'm a firm believer in children listening to their parents. Why don't you both go home, and I'll save you each a piece for your next visit. Or who knows—by then I may have baked something else! Zari!" she called.

Zari went into the passage, too, and put her shoes on. "Bye, Mrs Jamaica," she said. "Thank you."

"Goodbye, love," said Mrs Jamaica, giving her a hug.

"What's wrong with you?" Ekrem asked his sister

when they got outside.

"Nothing," answered Zari. "Why should there be?"

"Your eyes are red," Ekrem replied, smugly. "You've been crying, haven't you?"

"I have not!" Zari retorted. Well, she hadn't. Nearly, but not quite.

"Liar," said Ekrem.

"I'm not lying!" shouted Zari, as their mother answered the door.

"Zarifeh!" exclaimed her mother in a very stern voice. "There's no need to shout at your brother like that! And don't ever disappear without telling me where you're going, even if it's only next door!" Why was everybody angry at her today? Zari burst into tears and dashed up the stairs.

"Told you you've been crying!" Ekrem called up after her.

# Homework

The next day Sophie wasn't at school, but the new girl from over the road was. Zari had to sit next to her, but neither of them looked at each other the whole day, unless they had to. When the children went outside to play, a group of girls gathered around the new girl, but nobody gathered around Zari. Her memory heard Sophie shouting, "What other friends?" over and over and over. Maybe she didn't have any after all. But there was that new girl, eating everybody else's sweets, and they were just *giving* them to her. Zari thought she was going to be sick. She hoped the new girl was going to be, too.

After school, Zari went back to Mrs Jamaica's. She didn't race Ekrem up the stairs when she got home, but stalked up slowly and laid her satchel carefully on the bed. She didn't even stop to play with baby Ahmed. "I'm going to Mrs Jamaica's," she told her mother stiffly, and left.

Mrs Jamaica let her in without a word, and they both marched out to the kitchen. Mrs Jamaica got out two plates, two pieces of ginger cake, and two mugs. She put the cake on the plates and made tea in the mugs. She put lots of sugar in Zari's tea, just as Zari liked it.

They sat at the table quietly for a while. Zari leaned her elbows on the table and her head against her arm and stared at her cake. It looked soft and gooey and hardly any crumbs had fallen off.

"Well," said Mrs Jamaica finally. "Aren't you going to taste some and tell me how it is?"

Dutifully, Zari stuck a finger into the cake and pulled off a bit. It was delicious. Zari had never tasted ginger until she got to London, but after the first shock, she had realized it was a flavour she dearly loved. "It's good, Mrs Jamaica!" she exclaimed in spite of herself. "It's always good."

"I think you've got a story to tell me, my dear," said Mrs Jamaica.

Zari told her about her day at school—how there was a new girl and everyone wanted to talk to her and no one wanted to play with Zari.

"Why didn't you join everybody else to make her feel welcome? If you had done, soon you would have felt welcome, too," Mrs Jamaica suggested.

"She doesn't like me," Zari said.

"How do you know? You said she was new. How could she know if she liked you or not?"

Zari didn't say anything.

"Do you mean," Mrs Jamaica asked quietly, "that you don't like her?"

"No," said Zari stubbornly. "She doesn't like me. I sat next to her the whole day. She didn't say one word to me. She talked to everybody else."

"Did you say one word to her?"

Zari sighed. "No."

"Listen, darling," said Mrs Jamaica. She was putting on her very-patient voice, which she hardly ever used, and which Zari knew meant she was getting *im*patient. "When someone is new to a school, it isn't really up to them to make themselves feel welcome. Of course they need to try, just like you did when you first arrived in London. But it's the job of the children who are already there to make it easy for the new pupil to make friends. Are you making it easy?"

"I don't need to," Zari said. This conversation was stuck. She was wondering why she had come to Mrs Jamaica's at all. "Everybody else is making it easy for her. It won't make a difference if I do or not."

"It will make a difference to you," Mrs Jamaica said. "Especially when she's a Pakistani and she lives over the road and your best friend isn't talking to you right now."

Zari stopped staring at what was left of her cake, or at her tea, and stared at Mrs Jamaica. How did she know that? Maybe she had seen them yesterday after all. Or maybe she was magic.

Mrs Jamaica smiled. "Are you wondering how I knew that? It's easy; I knew a family had moved into that house, and I made them a cake."

Zari remembered when they had first moved in, Mrs Jamaica had made them a cake, too. Zari didn't know anyone else who did anything like that.

"While I was there," Mrs Jamaica was saying, "I asked them how they were settling in, and the father told me the children had had some trouble with other children in the neighbourhood that afternoon. I didn't want to think you had been the trouble, love, but after talking to you, I put two and two together and, well, am I right?"

Zari hung her head. "You're right," she muttered. Then it all spilled out. "I didn't want to play with them yesterday, because they're Pakis—I mean Pakistanis, sorry, Mrs Jamaica—and then I could see they felt bad, and it made *me* feel bad, but Sophie was so angry at me, and I didn't want her to win when she was being so awful so I kept being awful and then they went in and she went in and I went in—here. And then they put *that girl* in the seat next to me in school, and Sophie wasn't there, and everybody else paid attention to her and not to me, and—well, I already told you."

"I see," said Mrs Jamaica, as though she had seen it

all ages ago. "Do you have any homework tonight?"

Zari was bewildered. "What--?"

"Do you have any homework tonight?"

"A little—reading."

"All right then; pretend I'm a teacher, and I'm going to give you a little more."

Zari screwed up her face at that. Who ever heard of giving homework outside of school? And why should Zari do it?

"I want you to go home," Mrs Jamaica continued, "and think about one nice thing you can do to make Sajda feel welcome. Not just welcome at school, but welcome to our street. Welcome by *you*. And then you can come back here and tell me what you did and how it went, and if Sajda liked it."

There didn't seem to be anything else to say to Mrs Jamaica after that, and Mrs Jamaica clearly didn't have anything else to say to her. Zari finished her cake and her tea, and then went back home. She did her reading; it was a story about a genie in a magic lamp. Then Boba came home, and they had dinner, and drank sweet, dark, milk-less Albanian tea, which they only ever drank with other Albanians, and played card games. Zari made sure she did not think about anything nice she could do for Sajda.

Sophie was back in school the next day, but that made things even worse than the day before. She was keeping her word about not being friends with Zari, that was certain. She would walk past Zari in the school yard, her nose in the air and Sajda right beside her. Neither of them even gave Zari a glance. They were laughing and having a good time, but Zari was sure they laughed louder when she was near, just to annoy her. Well, it was working; she was very annoyed. But she tried not to show it, and went off to play with Ekrem and his friends.

"No girls allowed!" yelled Robert.

"Oh leave off!" said Ekrem. He didn't exactly want his little sister playing with him and his friends either, but he was loyal when one of his family members was in trouble, and he could tell Zari was. She got whiny often and cried a lot, and when that happened, he taunted her like he had two days ago. But whatever was bothering her this time had lasted three days. He thought it must be serious. She still hadn't told him what was wrong, but he knew she would eventually, and if she didn't, he was determined to find out.

Robert and the other boys groaned loudly, but they let Zari play. She surprised all of them, including herself, by being a better footballer than anyone had thought. She even scored a goal off of Robert, to his great embarrassment and to her enormous delight. Even Ekrem was proud of her. After that, the day wasn't so bad. She went home glowing, boasting to Noneh about her football victory, with Ekrem making suitable impressed-sounding noises in the background. When they got in the house, she was the first one in, the first one up the stairs, and her satchel landed on her bed first, too. "I won!" she crowed.

Then she went downstairs for a drink of juice. Anita was not there today, so Zari flopped on the settee where Anita normally sat, and drank her juice luxuriantly. Ekrem came in and changed the television channel to cartoons. Noneh stayed in the kitchen. After about half and hour, she poked her head in the door and asked, "Aren't you two going to go outside and play?"

"When Robert gets back," Ekrem said. "He has swimming lessons after school on Thursdays."

Zari didn't say anything. She felt like a cloud had just stationed itself in front of her sun, and it didn't look like it had plans to move any time soon. She didn't have plans to move either. She would just stay indoors for the rest of her life if she had to, rather than face Sophie and Sajda, or even Mrs Jamaica. She especially disliked thinking about Mrs Jamaica right now. She thought about the "homework" she hadn't done. The homework she would never do. She guessed even Mrs Jamaica would stop being her friend now.

# Albanian Music

*O*ne day when Noneh came to pick the children up from school, she didn't call, "Zarifeh!" as if she were angry, and she had a strange, secret smile on her face. Zari noticed it right away. "Noneh, what's happened? You look like a—like a cat that's caught a bird." Zari may not have seen Mrs Jamaica for a long time, but she still remembered some of that lady's descriptive phrases. They often involved cats.

Noneh just kept smiling as Ekrem and Zari pestered her all the way home. When they got to the door, they could hear music coming out of it. In fact, it seemed to be squeezing through the closed windows as well. When Noneh opened the door, the music positively poured out. "What is it?" Zari asked.

Noneh looked dismayed. "It's Albanian music,

Zarifeh. Don't you remember what your own music sounds like?"

"Yes," answered Zari quickly. "But we don't have any Albanian music." She would never admit it to her mother, but she probably would have indeed forgotten what "Albanian music" sounded like if it weren't for her friend, Lavdita, and her family from Prishtina, who were refugees in East London, too. They had a video player and their cousins sent them Albanian music videos sometimes.

"Well, we have now," replied Noneh proudly.

"Is it a cassette?" Ekrem asked, kicking off his shoes. So far the only way the family had to play music was through an old square black radio with a tape deck in it. Usually Agron was the one who used it. He borrowed cassettes from his friends in secondary school and played them very loudly at ten o'clock at night if his parents weren't home to tell him off on behalf of the neighbours. His friends' music had a lot of drums and noise and not much singing. Ekrem liked it, too. Zari pretended she liked it, and was beginning to convince herself. Jasmina never pretended any such thing and was very clear about the fact that she hated it.

"It's a kind of cassette, yes," Noneh answered, again with that secret smile on her face.

Zari peered into the sitting room and then hurtled into it with a yell. She had noticed three things all at once, and wasn't sure which pleased her most. The first thing was that Boba was home and not at work as usual. The second thing was sitting under their television—it was a video recorder. It glistened black and smooth, and the buttons just begged to be pushed. They had never had a video since they left Kosovo. Maybe they hadn't even had one in Kosovo, actually. Zari didn't remember. But they had one now, and the third delightful thing was that this wonderful new machine was playing an Albanian music video on their television.

She ran to Boba and threw her arms around his neck and kissed him. Then she ran to the machine and kissed it. Then she kissed the television. Then she stood up in the middle of the room, raised her arms up in the air, waving them round and round, swaying her hips back and forth, stepping small dainty steps with her feet in time to the music. Boba and Noneh laughed and laughed and laughed. Zari laughed, too.

Ekrem had been close on Zari's heels when she had catapulted into the sitting room. He didn't join in with her hugging and kissing and dancing, but he did yell a louder yell than even she had, and then he began bombarding his father with questions. "Why aren't you at work? Where did you get that? Where did the cassette come from? Does Agron know about it?" The only question he got an answer to at the time was the last one; Agron did not know about it. Ekrem let out another whoop. "Wait 'til he gets home!" he crowed.

"Wait 'til Jasmina gets home!" Zari echoed. "We'll

dance forever and ever!" Jasmina was a very good dancer, and she was beginning to teach Zari. Noneh laughed again and then disappeared into the kitchen as usual, to prepare dinner. Lavdita's family was coming over in the evening to celebrate the new machine and music with them; this dinner needed to be a special meal.

It was a lot like the meal Doruntina had prepared for them when they left Kosovo, Zari thought. She thought so every time her mother served it, which was at nearly every special occasion. When Ekrem had had his surgery and special ceremony that went with it, the party was at Lavdita's house, but Noneh made the same meal. When Jasmina turned eighteen, Noneh made it again. Zari asked Jasmina about this once. "I think it makes her feel like she's bringing home here," Jasmina had said.

Zari had a hard time remembering not to call England "home." Whenever Noneh said "home," everyone knew she meant Kosovo. Boba had been living in England so long, he sometimes forgot and called it "home." Whenever he did that, he would grin an impish grin and say, "Don't tell your mother!" Zari always got a little angry at him when he did that, but though she tried as hard as she could to remember that Kosovo was the real home, it was hard to feel like it most of the time.

Ekrem laughed at her when she talked to him about this. "Noneh's old," he said. "Anyway, she grew up in Kosovo, so of course it feels like home to her. But we aren't—we're growing up here. I like it here."

"Why?" Zari asked. "It always rains here, and the houses are too close together and the trees can't get out—"

"What do you mean the trees can't get out?" Ekrem asked. She had never talked to him about the sawn-off trees before. "Trees don't go anywhere."

"Forget it," said Zari. "Anyway, it's ugly and wet and grey and there are no mountains and the music is rubbish and nobody knows how to dance."

"You've been listening to Jasmina and Noneh too much," Ekrem said matter-of-factly. "The music is not rubbish—you like it yourself, and everybody knows how to dance—it's just different from Albanian dancing. And there are no football or cricket teams to support in Kosovo."

Zari had to agree with all these things, but she didn't say so. Instead, she simply said, "But there aren't enough Albanians here." The trouble was, when they were with other Albanians, it made Zari feel even worse.

Lavdita, her mother, her father, and her older brother came over to watch the new video on the new machine. They oohed and ahhed over it, even though they had had a video recorder for years and also had the very same video. They ate Noneh's feast enthusiastically, even though they had it at Zari's house nearly every time they visited. But they never let the juice run down their fingers. "It's because they're from Prishtina," Agron had told Zari once.

After the meal, Boba laughed and said, "Zari's learning how to dance. Show us, Zari!"

Zari giggled and got up and began to dance; she hoped she looked like the lady on the television screen. Her audience laughed and clapped along with her, and then suddenly Zari remembered that she had an audience. She giggled again with embarrassment and collapsed in a corner.

"Oh come, Zari!" urged Lavdita's mother, Zahe. "You were doing very well! Show us some more!"

But Zari grinned unhappily and shook her head. She loved her father, but she might not forgive him for making a spectacle out of her. Everyone had been laughing. Laughing at her. She just knew it.

Zahe was talking to her again. "You speak English very well now, don't you, Zari?"

Zari looked at her. She was afraid she knew what was going to happen. She wished she could go upstairs and hide under the bed or something. Why didn't somebody do something? Why didn't Jasmina change the subject? Why wouldn't Lavdita play with her? Why didn't they all watch the video again and forget about her?

"I don't know," Zari answered Zahe.

"I remember when you first got here, how long it took that child to learn *any* English," Zahe went on, speaking to Noneh and Boba now. "But now listen to her—chattering away to Ekrem in a foreign language as she's been doing all evening. I wouldn't be surprised if

60

she forgot her Albanian!"

Zari saw Noneh's face cloud over. She saw Boba squirm. She squirmed herself.

Suddenly Zahe was firing questions at her. All kinds of questions, silly questions, important questions, it didn't matter. They were all in Albanian, and Zari knew it was a test. Zahe wanted to show that Zari was forgetting her Albanian. Everyone was looking at her again.

Maybe if Zahe hadn't been a grown-up, Zari would simply not have answered. Maybe if Zahe had been from a village instead of from Prishtina, Zari would have laughed in her face. But she was a grown-up from Prishtina, and Zari didn't even feel as if she had a choice in the matter. She answered and answered and tried to keep the nervous shuddering out of her voice, and the pauses and English out of her sentences.

And then it happened. She forgot a word. As soon as she forgot it, she forgot which word she was trying to remember, and she just sat there, with a cold feeling in her stomach and a hot feeling in her face and her mouth hanging partly open. No one else said anything either, not even Zahe. But Zahe's lips were pursed together in a small smile that said, "It's just as I thought."

Suddenly Jasmina stood up. "Come on, everyone!" she said in a too-loud voice. "This is a good song. Let's all of us dance." There was a reluctant and uncomfortable shuffling as people got out of the chairs and settees and stood in an oval in the middle of the room, but it didn't take long for them to begin dancing in earnest. Soon everyone was laughing again, singing along with the lady on the video. Even Zari almost forgot the quiz of a few moments ago. She had thought she would escape upstairs when they all started dancing, but she hadn't been able to get to the door right away, and by the time she did, she was having fun, too. She didn't mind dancing with visitors as long as she wasn't the only one.

By the time Lavdita and her family left, it was midnight. "*Natone mir!*" they said to each other, shaking hands. The ladies kissed each other on both cheeks. "*Natone mir!* Good night!"

# *Shqip*

*A*fter school the next day, Zari went to Zahe's. She had never been there without her mother before, and she was nervous. At some point in the previous evening, Zahe and Noneh had had a talk. Noneh told Zari about it at breakfast. "Today you're going to Zahe's to learn *shqip*," she said.

Zari stared at her. "I already know Albanian," she said uncertainly. She thought she was going to cry.

Noneh noticed and came round to her chair to hug her. "Yes, you do," she said. "But you *are* forgetting, Zarifeh. We just don't want you to forget. It's very important to remember your country, even if you never see it again."

"What about Ekrem and Agron?" Zari asked. "They speak less *shqip* than I do. They forget words all the time."

Noneh's mouth got tight and for a second Zari thought Noneh was going to cry. Zari wished she hadn't said anything.

"They do forget," Noneh finally said sadly. "But they don't care. You care, I think, don't you, Zarifeh? You want to remember?"

"Of course I do, Noneh," Zari said, finally returning her mother's hug. "I'll practice *shqip* if you want me to. But Noneh, do I have to learn from Zahe?"

"I'm sorry, Zarifeh. But who else could teach you?" Noneh sighed.

"Jasmina?"

"She's too busy with her own studies, and you're sisters. You'd never learn anything—she'd let you get away with too much."

"Anita?"

"Anita hasn't offered. And her children are too small. It would be difficult for her to teach you and look after her children at the same time."

"Could you ask her, Noneh? Please?"

"It's time for school, Zarifeh."

Zari spent the entire day hoping her mother would ask Anita to teach her Albanian instead. But when Noneh came to pick her and Ekrem up at the end of the day, they walked away from home instead of to it. Zari knew they were going to Zahe's after all. Noneh knocked on the door. Lavdita answered it. "Hello!" she said, welcoming the three of them in. "I'll just get my mother."

Zahe came downstairs almost immediately, with a great smile. "Welcome!" she said. "Will you stay for a drink, first?"

Zari hoped Noneh would say yes, but it turned out later that the question was just politeness, and that actually Noneh and Zahe had arranged the night before that Zari would be at Zahe's on her own. "You are my friends and you are welcome at any time. You know that," Zahe had told Noneh. Ekrem had been eavesdropping and reported to Zari after her first lesson. "But," Zahe had continued, "when I am a teacher, I am a teacher, and I need to be with my pupils on their own."

So when Zahe asked if they wanted a drink that afternoon, Noneh already knew what to do, and said, "Thank you very much, Zahe. We will stop when we return to get her. I need to go to the shops. Good afternoon!"

"Good afternoon, then," said Zahe, as if she were surprised and a little disappointed. She closed the door, with Zari on one side of it and Noneh and Ekrem on the other side. Zari wondered if prison felt like this. They sat down at the table in the kitchen and Lavdita poured out three glasses of mango juice. It looked like Lavdita was going to stay with them, then, at least. Zari felt a little better.

"Now," said Zahe, after the three of them were settled around the table, "Zarifeh, have you got a notebook?"

Zari hadn't. "But I can get one tomorrow," she said, wondering where she would get the money. If it was money to help her improve her Albanian, and not just to buy a packet of crisps or something, surely her parents would give it to her? A notebook was expensive, though. It was worth about three or four packets of crisps.

"No need," Zahe said while Zari was working this out in her head. "Lavdita, please get Zarifeh a notebook."

Lavdita dragged a chair over to the small cupboard above the cooker. Zari was surprised to see, when she opened it, that the cupboard did not have food or kitchen things in it, as she would have expected. Instead, there was a small stack of notebooks and a tin which used to have olives in it but now was stuffed with pens and pencils instead. Lavdita took down a small notebook with a hot pink cover, and brought down the entire tin of pens and pencils.

"But," said Zari, "I could just borrow a piece of paper today and bring my own notebook tomorrow."

"It's no trouble," said Zahe. "As you can see, we have plenty of them. I just want to help you with your *shqip*. One notebook is very little to give, to help a child remain close to her own country."

Maybe Zahe was nicer than Zari had thought.

Lavdita opened her own notebook, which was green, and Zari opened her pink one. Two fresh white, blue-lined pages gleamed up at them. Zari ran her hand across the paper. She loved new notebooks. They were smooth and bright and fresh. In a few days, the pages would start to get bumpy with writing, and it was usually writing that

Zari would prefer not to be doing. Then she would get fed up with the book and try to lose it. But when it was new like this, it was exciting and Zari felt important. She looked at Zahe expectantly.

"All right," said Zahe in Albanian. "You both speak *shqip* fairly well. But I happen to know that neither of you know how to write it. I believe, Zarifeh, that no one has even taught you the alphabet?"

Zari looked puzzled. She knew the alphabet—but she had an idea that maybe Zahe was talking about something else.

"*Our* alphabet," Lavdita explained. "Not the English one."

"Oh," said Zari.

So Zahe began to teach them the alphabet. It had a lot more letters than the English one. "And each one always makes just its own sound," she explained to the two girls, "so it's much easier to spell—not crazy like English. In English, you can have 'ee' and 'ea' and 'y' and 'ie' and it might all sound the same, depending on the word. In *shqip*, all you have to write for that sound is 'i'." Zari was relieved. She hated spelling in school. She was terrible at it. Maybe she could actually spell if it was her own language, with a sensible spelling like this.

By the end of the lesson, the first page of Zari's notebook was covered with the Albanian alphabet. Zari reckoned she wouldn't need too many more lessons, now that she knew how to write all the sounds she had been speaking since she could talk. She thought she must know about all there was to know.

"I'm going to set you a homework," Zahe said. "When you go home, I want you to think of ten *shqip* sentences, and see if you can guess how to write them in our language, in our spelling. You can bring them back for your next lesson next week."

Boba and Noneh came round when the lesson was over, to collect Zari. "Come along, Zarifeh," said Noneh. "*Faleminderet*, Zahe. Thank you."

"Don't mention it," said Zahe. "And don't go just yet. As you're all here, why don't you stay for a while?"

Boba and Noneh both stepped inside and took their shoes off by the door. It was midnight again by the time they left, but Zari had fallen asleep on the settee long before that. Zahe's husband, Avni, gave them a lift home in his car, so Zari never woke up until her mother called her for school the next morning.

Zari had never been much of one for languages. At any rate, she hated studying English at school. "We can just speak it—why do we have to study it, too?" she often asked. But there was something exciting about having a new alphabet—her own alphabet, which even made sense. It was sort of like having a secret code. But secrets aren't much fun without someone to share them, and so Zari brought her notebook to school and practised what she knew by teaching the Albanian alphabet to her friend Gemma. Gemma, like some of the other girls, had gone back to being friends with Zari after Sajda stopped being new, which had only taken about a week and a half, so Zari wasn't lonely at lunch time any more, even when the boys didn't want her to join them.

Gemma and Zari practised Albanian sounds all day. Zari taught Gemma the sounds that went with each letter. Gemma helped pick out the sounds in words that Zari said to her, so that Zari could spell them better. Zari had completed her ten Albanian phrases in one lunch hour. So when her mother asked her, an hour before dinner, if she had any homework, she called cheerily, "No!" And then she stopped feeling cheery for the rest of the afternoon.

Homework. Her mother's question had reminded her of Mrs Jamaica. Again. Whenever someone said "homework" now, it felt as if strange little creatures had crawled inside Zari's stomach and were dancing there. Whenever she glimpsed Mrs Jamaica hanging up her washing in her back garden, Zari would always look away, or dash inside with a red face and an uncomfortable feeling in her shoulders. She imagined that Mrs Jamaica had put a spell on her to make her feel like that, but she knew it wasn't true. She had felt that way before, and it was always when she had done or was doing something wrong.

Today, the feeling was stronger than ever. "It's stupid," Zari told herself sternly. "Sajda isn't even new any more, and she's got Sophie to play with. She doesn't need me to be nice to her."

She remembered Mrs Jamaica saying that if she helped Sajda, she would help herself, too. "That's stupid, too," Zari said aloud. "How could it help me? Anyway, I don't need any help. I've got a friend now, and if I hadn't, I could always play football with the boys."

"What are you talking about?" Ekrem asked, looking away from the cartoons on the television with an annoyed expression on his face.

"What?" said Zari in surprise. "Oh! Did I say something?"

"Yes," said Ekrem. "You said something about stupid and needing help and playing football with the boys. Why *do* you play football with us, anyway, Zari? Do you fancy Robert or something?"

"Certainly not!" said Zari indignantly.

"You're turning red!" Ekrem crowed. "You do fancy him! Why did I never notice that before?" Ekrem completely forgot his cartoons. He flung himself onto the chair next to Zari so he could tease her more conveniently.

"I do not fancy Robert!" Zari exclaimed vehemently. A little too vehemently, she thought afterwards. She had fancied Robert ever since she scored that goal off of him, but she had no intention of letting anyone know it.

"Oh really?" Ekrem asked sceptically. "Then why are you turning redder than ever, and why are you shouting so loud?"

"Because you're bothering me," Zari said, a little more quietly. "Leave me alone."

"Girls are so moody," Ekrem said to himself. Then, turning back to his sister, he asked, "All right then, Miss Nun," (he had just been learning about Catholics in his Religious Education classes at school), "if you really don't fancy Robert, what are you doing playing football with us all the time, then?"

"I don't play football with you all the time," Zari countered. "I teach Gemma *shqip*, for one thing."

"Today's the first day you've ever done that," said Ekrem. "You barely even knew *shqip* before…"

"I did too know it!" Zari retorted. "Better than you, anyway, Mr English-person. You don't even remember what '*dashuri*' means!"

"How could I forget?" Ekrem asked. "It's in every single song in those new videos we've got. But even if I had forgotten it, I don't need to use it. I'm not the one who's in *love*!"

Zari sighed with irritation. She had hoped the subject had changed for good, but Ekrem had brought it right back where it had begun, and Zari didn't want to have to explain why she sometimes played football with the boys. It would be embarrassing either way. She would either have to admit that she liked Robert, or she would have to do what she had avoided doing for weeks, and tell Ekrem what had happened with Sophie and Sajda and Mrs Jamaica. She didn't know why she never wanted to tell him that. She was sure he would be on her side. Something inside her—maybe those dancing animals in her stomach—made her think she almost didn't want him to be on her side. She jumped up, pelted up the stairs, and slammed the door to her room.

Ekrem finished watching his cartoon.

But no one came over to visit that night, and so after dinner, when Zari went into hiding again, Ekrem followed her. She thought she might be sorry later, but she let him into her room.

"Okay, Zari," said Ekrem, flopping onto Jasmina's bed, across from where Zari sat on her own. There was none of this teasing business about Robert any more. Even Ekrem could tell that wasn't why Zari had run off on him and slammed the door earlier. "You've been keeping a secret for four weeks."

How did he know?

"We don't keep secrets from each other, do we, Zari? I always tell you all of mine."

"You do not," Zari pouted. "I haven't heard one of your secrets in my entire life."

Ekrem stopped and thought about this. "Okay, that's true," he admitted. "But you've always told me *your* secrets before and I haven't told anyone, have I?"

"So?" Zari asked. "Why should I tell you? You've never told me anything about you." She had never thought about this, but now she realised it could be an important point. It made her wonder why she had ever told him anything. He didn't deserve it, did he? Well, she didn't have to tell him this. She wasn't going to.

"Oh, come off it, Zari." Ekrem realized he had made a mistake. She might never talk to him now that she thought he owed her a few secrets. But he was going to try to get her to anyway. "I don't have to—I'm your brother. You know everything about me already; girls understand what's going on with people so much better than boys. If I had any secrets, I would tell you, definitely."

"Oh right," said Zari, in a voice that meant she didn't believe him. Her bed was next to the window, and she turned her back toward her brother and rested her elbows on the window sill. It was still light out, even though it was half past eight. Summer holidays were coming, and Zari would have to keep playing football with the boys. Gemma lived too many streets away; Zari's parents wouldn't let her walk that far on her own every day. She watched the sky turn red and golden and purple.

"I would, I would!" Ekrem promised. "Um—if I could think of any right now, I would tell you." He sat quiet for a minute, thinking. Then he said, "Look, Zari, I just want to help you. You don't have to tell me anything, of course, but wouldn't you feel better if you talked about it? I know you and Sophie aren't friends any more and you never go to see Mrs Jamaica. What happened?"

Zari turned sideways and lay back on her pillow. "I don't think I'll feel better if I tell anyone," she said. "I think I'll just feel bad forever."

Ekrem felt sorry for his sister. He wanted to help her. He wanted her to get her friends back, and he, too, knew that if she didn't, she'd be playing football with him and his friends all summer. But she was acting ridiculously, and he had had enough. "Fine!" he said, getting up. "Be that way. Feel bad forever—but it won't be my fault!"

It wasn't until Ekrem left that Zari realized something. She wasn't able to talk to anyone, now that she couldn't talk to Mrs Jamaica. She had never confided much in Noneh, even though she loved her dearly, because Noneh got nervous and worried so easily. She had never confided in Boba, even though she loved him, too, because she thought he might laugh at her. She had never confided in Agron because he was too old and he was a boy. But she had always told Jasmina everything, and Ekrem everything else. Yet somehow, now that she didn't have Mrs Jamaica to talk to any more, she couldn't talk to them either.

This puzzled Zari. She didn't know why she even liked to talk to Mrs Jamaica. Mrs Jamaica saw things differently, and usually the way she saw them was in a way that Zari didn't like. Like imagining she could do something nice for Sajda.

What would it be like, Zari wondered. She could go to school on Monday and say, "Hello, Sajda," and she could offer her some of her crisps. Sajda would be so surprised! She would stare and stammer and then she'd have to take the crisps because she wouldn't know what else to do. And Sophie! Sophie wouldn't know what to do either.

Zari frowned. Sophie would probably know just what to do. She would tease. She would remind Sajda that Zari was a bigot. She would say, "Hey, Zari, what are you trying to get, being all nice all of a sudden? Did all your other friends leave you, too?"

Zari crawled under her duvet with the light still on and thought about this. It wasn't worth it—trying to be nice to Sajda. And she really didn't need to be. All of them had their own friends now. They didn't need to be friends all together. She was not going to do Mrs Jamaica's homework.

The next day was Saturday. Mrs Jamaica came over with a cake.

Mrs Jamaica hadn't come over since the day she had set Zari that homework, and Noneh hadn't gone to Mrs Jamaica's either. She had been busy, and had been enjoying the Albanian videos. Besides all that, she knew that something had happened between Zari and Mrs Jamaica. She didn't know what but she didn't want to visit anyone who had hurt her daughter's feelings. She was very surprised to see Mrs Jamaica on her doorstep.

"Hello," said Noneh. "Come in."

"Thank you," replied Mrs Jamaica, extending her cake. "I made this for you and your children. I haven't seen any of you in ages, and I didn't think that seemed right, our being neighbours and all."

Noneh looked embarrassed. Maybe Mrs Jamaica was angry that they hadn't come over.

"I don't think that's what she means, Noneh," Zari whispered from the sitting room in Albanian. "I think she just misses us." And then she startled herself, because suddenly she was flying across the sitting room and giving Mrs Jamaica a big hug. "I missed you, too, Mrs Jamaica," she said in English. She didn't know how much she had missed her until that second.

"Why didn't you come over then, child?" asked Mrs Jamaica softly, as if Noneh and Jasmina weren't in the room. But she put a finger over Zari's lips before Zari could answer. "Come over tomorrow when I get home from church, and tell me, yeah? In the meantime, I have other gossip to attend to. I hear through the grapevine that there's talk of Jasmina getting married." She settled herself down on the settee between Jasmina and Zari.

Noneh looked puzzled. Her English still wasn't very good. Jasmina translated. Zari wondered if there was a grapevine she hadn't noticed between her family's back garden and the Jamaicas'. Did grapes grow in England? And how could Mrs Jamaica have heard anything through them? She was too busy thinking about this to listen to Jasmina's translation and see if it made more sense in Albanian.

But Noneh was listening, and when Jasmina blushed at the end of it, Noneh smiled. "Ah," she said, as if she had plenty to tell. "One moment please." She bustled off to the kitchen and returned with cold drinks on a tray for everyone, and a bowl of biscuits. Then she sat down on the floor by the settee and smiled. "Yes," she said, English sounding awkward in her mouth, "Jasmina getting married."

"They haven't decided for certain," Jasmina said quickly, in both English and Albanian.

"Zari surprised," Noneh said, still smiling.

"No, I'm not!" Zari exclaimed indignantly. As if she hadn't overheard the talk among the grown-ups late at night for the last two months! "I've known about it for ages."

"Clever girl," Noneh said, for once not bothered about her daughter's eavesdropping. She turned back to Mrs Jamaica. "Nice boy," she said. Then she corrected herself, "Nice *man.*"

"How do you know him?" Mrs Jamaica asked.

"Cousin of friend Zahe," Noneh answered briefly. "Good boy. Good job."

"And he's Albanian, of course?"

"Of course," Noneh laughed.

"What religion is he?" Mrs Jamaica asked, as if she were just making conversation. But Zari saw Jasmina stiffen. She wondered at this. There was something Mrs Jamaica was asking that she wasn't actually saying, and Zari couldn't guess what it was.

"Muslim, of course," Noneh answered. She looked surprised, too, but more at the fact that anyone would have to ask what religion a Kosovar Albanian was, than at the question itself.

"Ah, Muslim," Mrs Jamaica said, taking a sip of her drink. "Is he very, well, religious?"

Noneh looked as if she felt a little guilty. "Like us," she said.

"I see," Mrs Jamaica responded. "So he's quite open to knowing other people of other religions, too, is he?"

Jasmina translated this, very stiffly, and with a white face. Noneh looked puzzled. Asking someone's religion was a general conversational question, if you were interested in that sort of thing, but it surprised her that Mrs Jamaica would go on and on about it like this.

"He like us," Noneh said again. "You, Christian; we, Muslim. Still friends."

"Yes," Mrs Jamaica relaxed a bit and smiled. "Of course we're still friends." Then she got serious again. "But I love Jesus very much, and if one day my daughter came home and told me she had become a Muslim, I would be very sad, even though many of my friends are Muslim."

Zari wondered if Mrs Jamaica's daughter had done just that, and what Jasmina's getting married had to do with it. She wondered why Mrs Jamaica would be sad if her daughter became a Muslim. Didn't she want her daughter to know the truth? Of course Mrs Jamaica loved Jesus, but she wouldn't have to stop loving him if she were a Muslim. Zari was Muslim, and she liked Jesus pretty well. She knew lots of stories about him from her Religious Education classes at school, and from school assemblies at Easter and Christmas. In fact, she would never tell anyone this, but she liked him rather better than Mohammed, even though she knew Mohammed was the greatest and final Prophet. Mrs Jamaica didn't have to worry if her daughter had become a Muslim—she could still love Jesus, but have Mohammed, as well.

Noneh looked like she thought Mrs Jamaica's daughter's becoming a Muslim might be a good thing, too, but she asked kindly, "Mrs Jamaica, your daughter married Muslim?" She seemed to understand the connection between this conversation about religion and the one about Jasmina's marriage. She said in Albanian, for Jasmina to translate, "Don't worry, we are careful to see that our daughter marries a Muslim. This is why arranged marriages are good."

"That's what I thought," Mrs Jamaica said, as if Noneh had set her mind at rest. She never answered the question about her own daughter. "But I have another question. We talked about how I would feel if my daughter became a Muslim; I would be very sad. I might even be angry. But of course I would still love her. I would never agree with her, but she would still be welcome in my home. What would you do if someone in your family decided they wanted to become a Christian?"

This time Noneh turned white. Zari could see she wanted to give a nice, gentle answer, and an angry, harsh answer at the same time, but instead she was honest, and simply said, "I don't know."

"I've upset you," Mrs Jamaica said with concern. "Please forgive me. It's just something to think about. And now, back to Jasmina's wedding. When is it going to be?"

They hadn't set a date yet. Mrs Jamaica started asking about the traditional Albanian wedding celebration, and Zari got bored. She went up to her room to draw pictures in her *shqip* notebook, which was the only one she had with a lot of blank pages left. She drew brides and grooms and flowers. The brides and grooms all had big eyes and short noses and she wasn't happy with any of them. She couldn't stop thinking about Mrs Jamaica's question. What would happen if someone in her family became a Christian? But no one would be silly enough to do that; no one in her family anyway.

# English Sunday Dinner

**N**ext afternoon, Zari went over to Mrs Jamaica's as soon as she heard her and her husband get home from church. She wanted to apologize for not doing her homework, and she wanted to talk to Mrs Jamaica about yesterday's question.

Mr Jamaica answered the door. "Hiya, Zari! You all right?" he asked, smiling a big smile and rumpling her curls. Zari didn't like when grown-ups patted her on the head. She wished she were taller so they would stop. But Mr Jamaica was nice, as far as she could tell, and he seemed truly happy to see her, so she forgave him. "I'm fine, thanks," she answered politely. "How are you?"

"Just fine, just fine," he laughed. "My wife said you might be coming over. She's just in the kitchen getting our dinner. If you're lucky, she might give you some, too."

In the kitchen, it looked like Mrs Jamaica was cooking for a party. "Are you having guests?" Zari asked uncertainly. Maybe this was a bad time to be here. Maybe she should come back later.

"Just you," Mrs Jamaica replied.

"But," protested Zari, "I don't eat very much; I could never eat all that!"

Mrs Jamaica laughed as if Zari had just said something especially funny, and Zari giggled a bit, too, even though she didn't know what was so amusing. "I don't expect you to eat all this, love," Mrs Jamaica said. "I always make a lot of food for Sunday afternoons."

"Why?" asked Zari.

"Used to just be tradition," Mrs Jamaica explained. "I was brought up that way. Even if we had less that a mouse-handful to eat during the week, my mother always made sure we had a feast on Sunday. It was a regular thing. Now that I'm grown up, I know I don't have to do it like that, but I also know Jesus better now, and having a feast seems like a good way to celebrate His special day after all, so I keep doing it. Besides, then we have leftovers and I hardly need to cook for the rest of the week."

Mrs Jamaica had the strangest way of talking about her Prophet. No one talked about Mohammed like that. It didn't seem very respectful, somehow. It sort of reminded Zari of the imaginary friend that she used to have before she met Sophie. Her imaginary friend had been an Albanian girl just like her, but with straight hair. Her name was Gona, just like Zari's sister who was still in Kosovo, and she always did everything Zari wanted her to. Even Ekrem didn't find out about Imaginary-Gona, because Zari never needed her when he was around. Zari thought maybe Mrs Jamaica needed Jesus because Mr Jamaica was at work so much during the week. But Mr Jamaica was home today, and here was his wife, still talking about Jesus as if he was here and Mr Jamaica wasn't.

"Of course, when you're celebrating," Mrs Jamaica went on, "you just want to celebrate and not have to work too hard, either, so mostly I get everything ready on Saturday night, except the vegetables. Then when I get home from church, the only one who's got to do any work is the cooker!" As she said this, she put a couple of saucepans with various vegetables in them, on the stovetop. There was already the smell of a chicken roasting in the oven.

She sat down at the kitchen table and patted the chair next to her for Zari to sit in. "So, darling. Tell me how you've been."

"Fine," said Zari. It was so strange. She thought she had so much to talk about, and now that she was here, she was shy and everything seemed a bit stupid, and she didn't want to tell Mrs Jamaica anything at all.

"That's good," Mrs Jamaica said. "I'm glad to hear it."

Then they were both quiet. The clock ticked. The oven made warm electrical noises as the chicken roasted inside it. Finally Zari blurted out, "Mrs Jamaica, you know that homework you set for me. Well, I didn't do it."

"I know," Mrs Jamaica said. "I was hoping you would, but never mind. Is that why you haven't been to see me all these weeks?"

"Yes." Zari hung her head.

"Don't be ashamed about *that* bit!" Mrs Jamaica exclaimed. "You don't *have* to come over here ever, although I like when you do. It makes me feel like I have a granddaughter, since my own daughter isn't doing much about giving me one herself!" She chuckled. Zari looked up again. She didn't normally notice things that people didn't come right out and say. But she heard in Mrs Jamaica's chuckle that Mrs Jamaica was sad, really; she wanted grandchildren a lot. And if her daughter wasn't doing much to give her one, it must mean she wasn't getting married after all, to a Muslim or anyone else. This reminded Zari of something.

"Mrs Jamaica," she began, "Why did you ask that question yesterday?"

"What question?" Mrs Jamaica wondered.

"The question about what Noneh would do if someone in the family became a Christian?"

"Oh, that. I just thought it was a good question to ask, that's all. It's always good to think about."

Zari was hearing all kinds of things she didn't normally hear today. Mrs Jamaica was lying. There was another reason she had asked that question. But Mrs Jamaica wouldn't lie, would she? If she had been talking to Ekrem, Zari would have called him a liar to his face and plagued the life out of him until he changed his story. Sometimes she called him a liar even when he was telling the truth, if she didn't like what the truth was. But Zari didn't know what to do when Mrs Jamaica was the one who was lying. So she said, "Your daughter's not really marrying a Muslim, is she?"

"No, she isn't," said Mrs Jamaica. "That was just an example."

They were quiet again for a minute. Some of what Zari was feeling must have flitted across her face, because finally Mrs Jamaica said, "I'm sorry, Zari. I wasn't being very honest right now."

Zari was startled again. She had never heard a grown-up admit they were wrong before, and she had certainly never heard one apologize for it. Maybe it meant Mrs Jamaica was weak. Yet somehow Zari didn't think it did. She didn't say anything.

Mrs Jamaica said, "I had other reasons for asking that question. But you'll have to trust me when I say I can't tell you what they are right now, and leave it with the reason I gave you. It *is* a good question to think about, you know. People do change their beliefs."

"But Mrs Jamaica, sorry, no offence. But why

would anyone in my family become a Christian? We're Muslim."

"I know you are, honey," Mrs Jamaica said. "But why are you Muslim?"

That question was almost stranger than the one about what Noneh would do if someone in the family stopped being a Muslim. Zari didn't know how to answer. "Because—because we are. Because we're Albanian. Because my Noneh and Boba are," she fumbled.

"Let me tell you a story, Zari," Mrs Jamaica offered. "I'm going to tell you about when I changed my beliefs. Is that okay with you?"

Mrs Jamaica had changed her beliefs? Zari wanted to hear about this! She wondered what she had been before, if she hadn't always been a Christian. What religion were people in Jamaica? "It's okay with me," Zari answered.

"Thank you," said Mrs Jamaica, settling herself more comfortably in her chair. "When I was a little girl, my family was Christian, just like yours is Muslim. We went to church every Sunday and had a big meal afterwards, like I was telling you when you came in. We celebrated Christmas and Easter, but you know what? We had no idea why we were doing it."

Zari thought about that. She and her family didn't even do so much as go to the mosque; but at least that way they didn't have to think about why they went or not. They celebrated the two most important Eids, though, and they even gave each other presents at Christmas and chocolate eggs at Easter, like the Christians did. With Christmas and Easter and two Eids as well, it made for a lot of presents during the year. Zari wasn't sure what they had to do with anything, but she liked them.

Mrs Jamaica went on. "Well, I was sort of a curious little girl, and so it wasn't long before I began to ask why we were doing all these things. At first my mother tried to make up her own answers, but I soon guessed that she didn't really know what she was talking about, and she realized that. Finally she got fed up with my asking and told me to stop. I stopped asking the questions out loud, but she couldn't keep me from asking them inside myself, and by the time I was a teenager, I had a list of them from here to Jamaica!"

Zari's eyes widened. She didn't think even she could come up with so many questions.

"The problem was," Mrs Jamaica said, "since no one would give me any answers, I thought there weren't any. So I kept asking the questions to myself and getting more and more fed up with church and finally I stopped going altogether. Then I met Mr Jamaica." Here she smiled. Zari squirmed. She hadn't expected a love story to come into this. She secretly liked love stories, but she never knew how to look or act while she was listening to them. She didn't want anyone to think she cared about them too much.

Mrs Jamaica noticed Zari's uneasiness, grinned some more, and went on. "Well now, I thought he was pretty nice, but you know what? He wouldn't even look at me."

Zari tried hard not to be interested, but she didn't think it was very kind of Mr Jamaica to ignore Mrs Jamaica. Maybe he wasn't as good as she had thought. "Why wouldn't he?" Zari asked.

"Because I wasn't a Christian," Mrs Jamaica answered simply.

"But you *were* a Christian!" Zari protested. "You just said—you went to church and everything. And anyway, you're good, so who cares?"

"Mr Jamaica cared," said Mrs Jamaica, "And believe me, darling, I wasn't all that good back then! Sure, I was religious, up until I stopped going to church. I knew all the answers to the questions I was allowed to ask in Sunday school, and I knew the Lord's Prayer and the Ten Commandments forwards and backwards."

Zari didn't know what the Lord's Prayer and the Ten Commandments were, but she didn't say so.

"I was religious," Mrs Jamaica repeated. "But I wasn't a Christian. Do you know what a Christian is, Zari?"

Zari was going to say yes, she did, but then she thought of all the people she knew and had heard of who called themselves Christians. She thought about Boba's saying, "There are Christians and there are Christians." He had explained what different Christians acted like, but he never told her what they actually were. "I don't know," she said.

"A Christian," said Mrs Jamaica happily, as if this were the point she had been waiting to make all along, "is someone who knows and loves Jesus. Someone who knows that they can never be good enough to get to God on their own, but they believe that Jesus will give them his goodness, and he died to take the punishment for their badness. He came back to life again, and if we trust him to get us to God (because he *is* God, really), he will. We can know him and love him and talk to him, and..."

Zari began squirming again. She had heard that Christians believed Jesus was God, or the Son of God, or something, but she had never heard one of them come out and say it before. She was surprised lightning didn't come down and strike Mrs Jamaica dead on the spot. But maybe Mrs Jamaica was good enough in other ways for God to make an exception for her, even though she had such terrible ideas about one of his Prophets. Only hadn't Mrs Jamaica just said something about not being good enough? And hadn't she said something like that before? But surely she was wrong about that, too. *Somebody* had to be good enough, even if they didn't think they were—otherwise Paradise would be pretty empty, and what a waste of time for God that would be!

"Anyway," Mrs Jamaica was coming back to herself, "I finally found all that out. I chased Mr Jamaica to his church, because I was interested in him, but the more I kept going, the more I became interested in Jesus instead. The reverend at that church was different from mine; he spoke as if he really knew what he was talking about. Finally one day I just couldn't stand it any longer; I had to know Jesus like that. So I talked to the reverend myself, and he prayed with me, and then I prayed, and for the first time in my life I actually felt like I was talking to a Real Person when I prayed. After that, I got baptised, and then, even though I had almost forgotten about him, Mr Jamaica started chasing *me*!" She chuckled. "So I got a God and a husband in the same year. It was a pretty good deal, I think."

Zari thought it was a little over the top, personally, but she didn't say so. She was trying to remember what had got Mrs Jamaica telling this story in the first place. Jasmina, and—oh! Was Mrs Jamaica trying to tell her that she had better get to know her religion a little better, too, just as Mrs Jamaica had got to know hers? Zari asked her.

Mrs Jamaica looked serious and shook her head. "Actually, Zari, what I'm saying is that no religion is enough. Not even Christianity if you don't know what (or who) it's about. And what that has to do with the questions I asked you before is, sometimes people, no matter what their religion, find out that Jesus is still a real live Person, and He's the only way to God. Then they have to change their loyalty forever, and it doesn't matter what country they come from. One day you may know someone who changes that way, too."

Zari didn't like this conversation. She wondered for

the millionth time why she kept going to the Jamaica's when it made her feel so uncomfortable. The only other thing she could think of to talk about was how she hadn't once tried to be nice to Sajda. That wasn't comfortable, either, and so she said nothing.

Mrs Jamaica took a deep breath and stood up. "Well!" she said. "I dare say these vegetables are done. Especially after all my talking!"

Zari helped Mrs Jamaica carry bowls and platters of things out to the dining room and put them on the table. The table had a plastic cover on it, but it had a design in it that was meant to look like lace, and Zari thought it was quite nice. "Would you call Mr Jamaica?" Mrs Jamaica asked Zari, even though he probably could have heard her, sitting in the next room as he was.

"Mr Jamaica!" Zari said, putting her head through the door and seeing that he was watching Wimbledon tennis on television, "It's time for dinner."

Mr Jamaica got up immediately. "There's only one thing that can tear me away from tennis," he grinned, "and that's Mrs Jamaica's cooking!" The three of them sat down around the table. Zari began to reach for the platter of chicken, but suddenly she felt both her hands gently clasped. She looked up, startled. Mr and Mrs Jamaica were holding hands, and with their free ones, they had each grasped one of Zari's. Their eyes were closed and their faces were pointed down at the table. "Lord," Mr Jamaica was saying, "Thanks for all this. We know we have so much compared to other people. Please take care of them, too, and don't let us forget to be thankful. In Jesus' Name we pray, amen." They opened their eyes and lifted their heads, and Zari's hands were free again.

"Help yourself!" said Mrs Jamaica. "It's a traditional English Sunday dinner, I think. I didn't feel like making anything Jamaican this week."

Zari discovered that day that English Sunday dinners were very nice, that Mr Jamaica was very funny, and that she didn't always have to have uncomfortable conversations in that house. But she never did talk about Sajda.

The next day, when she sat next to Sajda in school, she said, "Hiya, Sajda."

Sajda looked at her, startled, and mumbled, "Hello." Neither of them said anything to each other for the rest of the day, but it was a start.

# Sokol

One Friday, when Zari had her usual *shqip* lesson, it turned out not to be so usual after all. Noneh took her to Zahe's house after school as usual, but when they got there, she went into the house with Zari, instead of going back home. This was because someone besides Lavdita was in the sitting room. Zari looked at Noneh questioningly, but it was Zahe, still standing in the doorway who spoke. "How would you like to meet your new brother, Zarifeh?" she asked.

Zari was puzzled. She had learned something in school about how babies were made, and she hadn't noticed Noneh looking like she was going to have one. Besides, if Noneh *were* going to have a baby, Zari thought she should have had the decency to tell her herself, instead of letting Zahe do it.

Both Noneh and Zahe laughed, and Zari realised she had accidentally been scowling at Noneh's tummy while she was thinking this. She looked away, embarrassed.

"Not there," chuckled Zahe.

"Not that kind of brother," laughed Noneh. "Look— over there."

For the first time, Zari looked properly at the person sitting on the settee across from Lavdita. It was a young man, older than Agron, and taller, too, with straight, black hair and laughing black eyes. He stood up as Zari and Noneh came forward, greeting Noneh respectfully. Then he looked at Zari, and squatted down so that those eyes of his were on the same level as hers. He reached out, took her hand, and shook it. "Hello, Zarifeh," he said. He had a nice voice. Zari thought maybe if he sang, he would sound like one of the men on the *shqip* videos. "I'm Sokol. I've heard a lot about you. I'm so glad to finally meet you."

Zahe started saying something about how this was her cousin and he was going to marry Zari's sister, Jasmina, but Zari was hardly listening. She kept staring at Sokol. He was so handsome. She didn't think she had ever seen anyone so handsome before. She thought if she had been Jasmina, she would have been behaving a lot more excitedly than Jasmina actually was. Suddenly she heard everyone, including Lavdita, and even Sokol, laughing again. She blinked and realised Zahe had just said, "Look, Sokol, the younger one fancies you, too!"

"I do not!" Zari said, in *shqip*, which made them all laugh even more, though they raised their eyebrows in surprise and pleasure at the fact that she had answered in Albanian. She didn't even blush. But she did fancy Sokol—she knew it. Robert could play football by himself, for all she cared. She'd never fancy him again.

The *shqip* lesson that night lasted much longer than usual, and it wasn't really a lesson. Zari had been required to show off a little of her *shqip* to Sokol, but she wasn't nervous, because it was Sokol and because she knew *shqip* pretty well now, she reckoned. He smiled at her and nodded and made appreciative noises. Zari thought he was nothing like her real brothers—they would have acted bored and snorted at her.

But then Lavdita's brother got home, and Sokol left with him in his big noisy car. "Where are they going?" Zari asked, even though she knew Lavdita's brother went out to clubs every night. She didn't think Sokol would do a thing like that. He was nice, and he was going to marry her sister, Jasmina. "Out," answered Zahe simply. "In English they say, 'Boys will be boys,' and so they will."

She and Noneh started talking to each other about grown-up wedding things after that, and Zari got bored, so she and Lavdita went upstairs to Lavdita's room and talked and giggled themselves. "So," Lavdita asked her, "what do you think of your new brother?"

"I wish he wasn't going to be my brother," Zari said, "because then I could marry him myself!"

Lavdita laughed. "You're too young. Even *I'm* too young—or *I'd* marry him *my*self!"

"You couldn't," Zari countered, self-satisfied.

"Why not?" asked Lavdita, still laughing.

"Because he's your cousin. You can't marry your cousin!"

"He's my mother's cousin," Lavdita corrected her. "And anyhow, I could so marry him, even if he was my cousin—Albanians can."

Zari couldn't argue about this; she didn't understand enough about it. All she knew was that once, a long time ago, when she and Sophie had still been friends, they had had a discussion about marrying relatives. Sophie had told her it couldn't be done, and had been so certain of it that Zari had been convinced. But maybe Lavdita was right. Maybe there were different rules for Albanians. Zari would have to ask someone about this later. In the meantime, it was more fun talking about Sokol. Zari and Lavdita whispered and giggled about him—and Robert, and someone Lavdita fancied at school, too, just for good measure—until Noneh called that it was time to go home.

Zahe rarely fed them anything but tea and biscuits, so it was a late dinner when Zari and her mother got home. "I met your boyfriend!" Zari crowed to Jasmina when she saw her. Sokol couldn't really be considered Jasmina's boyfriend, since they had never "gone out" the way boyfriends and girlfriends were supposed to do in

England, but Zari knew her sister would be scandalised by the word, and thought it would be fun to tease her. But Jasmina just smiled distantly and didn't act shocked at all.

Zari would have tried a little harder to irritate her if she could have, but she was too tired. It must have been all that *shqip* she had been speaking earlier. As soon as dinner was over, she stumped upstairs to bed. Jasmina followed her. Zari thought that was a bit funny. Usually she was the one following Jasmina around. She thought maybe Jasmina wanted to talk to her about Sokol after all. Maybe she just hadn't wanted Noneh to hear anything. But she never mentioned him. Instead, she asked, "Zari, what did you talk about at the Jamaica's on Sunday?"

Zari stopped to think about it. At first all she could remember was Mr Jamaica's jokes, especially this one about a frog... Then she remembered sitting in the kitchen before dinner. Somehow, Zari knew this was the conversation Jasmina wanted to know about. She wondered why she hadn't asked her before.

"We talked about when Mrs Jamaica changed her beliefs, or something like that," Zari answered. "At least, that's what she called it. I don't think she had any beliefs before, really."

"Oh, right." Jasmina seemed relieved.

"Why?" Zari wanted to know.

"Oh—I was just wondering."

Zari thought of something else. "I asked her why she asked what Noneh would do if someone in our family became a Christian, but she wouldn't tell me. At first she said because it was a good question to think about, like she said while she was here, but then she said she was lying, and there was another reason but she wouldn't tell me what it was. Why do *you* think she asked?"

"I don't know," Jasmina said. Zari could tell she was lying, too, but she loved Jasmina too much to pester her like she would pester Ekrem about the same thing. Besides, just like Mrs Jamaica, Jasmina hardly ever lied, so she must have a good reason when she did it. Zari sighed and lay back on her pillow on the bed, with her hands behind her head. She wished she had a big fat pillow with pink frills around it. Her pillow was flat and the pillowcase was sort of a greyish white and very boring. But she could imagine she had a nice pillow instead. She sighed again, pretending, and wiggled her toes.

"What would *you* do if someone in this family became a Christian?" Jasmina asked curiously.

"I don't know," Zari answered carelessly. She was getting a little tired of the question. It didn't seem to have any point. It may be good to think about, she mused, but if you do it too long or too often, you get fed up. "What would you do?" she asked back.

Jasmina looked a little surprised, and then leaned back on her bed, too, and said, "I guess I don't know either. It would probably depend a little on whether I was the only other person in the family who knew, or if everyone did."

"What would you do if you were the only one?" Zari asked. She hadn't thought about it from that angle.

"Well, I would certainly keep it a secret, for one thing," Jasmina answered firmly. "I don't know how I would feel myself, but I don't think it's worth it to get the whole family upset at one person, just because they happen to start to believe something."

"What do you mean start to believe something?" Zari asked indignantly. It was her own sister, but it sounded as if she were insulting the family.

"Oh come on, Zari. You know no one in this family takes our religion very seriously."

"Noneh does."

"Noneh doesn't eat pork or drink alcohol. Neither do I. That doesn't mean she believes."

Zari wanted to know what it did mean then. "Don't you believe?" she asked.

"What about you, Zari?" Jasmina didn't answer the question. "What do you know about Islam?"

"I know," Zari said, "that Mohammed was the last and greatest Prophet, and God—I mean, Allah—made the angel Gabriel speak the Qur'an to him, and he wrote it all down, even though he couldn't read and write. I know the Qur'an is all the words of Allah, and the Bible has loads of mistakes in it (even though it has some nice stories in it, too; they told us some in R.E.). I know that only Muslims are going to go to Paradise if we're really really good."

"Do you think you're really really good?" Jasmina asked, laughing. "I love you, Zari, but I'm sorry, I don't think you are!"

Zari laughed, too, but her laughs immediately turned into a pout. "Come off it, Jasmina, you're starting to sound just like Mrs Jamaica."

"I thought you liked Mrs Jamaica," Jasmina grinned.

"I do," sighed Zari. "But every time I go over there, I find out I'm doing something wrong. It's really aggravating." Zari's teacher liked to use the word "aggravating," and so Zari had got in a habit of saying it, too.

"What do you keep going there for, then?"

Zari sighed for the fourth time in half an hour. She thought about how she was doing very well now at saying hello to Sajda in the mornings, although they still never said any more to each other than that. She wondered if Mrs Jamaica would think she was being kind enough. "I have no idea," she said, in answer to her sister's question.

Jasmina laughed again, reaching across the space between their beds and patting Zari's cheek. "You're cute," she said. Only Jasmina could get away with calling Zari cute.

"I love you, Jasmina," Zari said suddenly, sitting up and giving her a hug, and a kiss on the cheek.

Jasmina swallowed. Zari thought she should have said I love you, too, but when she looked at her face, she saw that her eyes were wet. Probably she had been about to cry and so hadn't been able to say anything. Jasmina was almost grown up now, and she cried a lot more than she used to. Why were grown-ups always so mushy? All Zari had done was given her sister a hug and a kiss. And said that she loved her.

# Summer Holidays

Zari was in the back garden, taking the washing off the line. School was out for the summer. Neither Zari nor Ekrem nor Agron were enrolled in any of the summer programmes that the borough council offered for children during the holidays, even though most of their friends were. Boba said it was too expensive. He said he could only afford to send one of them, and if he did that, he'd hear about it from the other two all summer. Zari secretly knew he was right, and Ekrem probably did, too, though they both assured their father that *they* at least would never make any trouble for him. They swore the same thing to each other, but neither of them meant it.

Unfortunately, Boba refused to listen to their perfectly reasonable arguments, and so they were stuck at home while their friends all learned to play football better, or take clever photographs, or ride horses, and then come back in the afternoons and brag about it. The one compensation Boba had allowed his younger children was that they were now permitted to walk to the next street on their own and play with their friends there, once those friends got home. If Agron or Jasmina went with them, they were also allowed to walk to the park. But Agron had gone out with friends today, so Zari couldn't go to the park. And Gemma wasn't coming home today; she was going to visit her grandmother in Surrey for the weekend, so Zari couldn't go to the next street. It left her with nothing to do but take the washing off the line. She was doing it as slowly as possible. She had nothing to look forward to, after all.

Noneh was the one who had asked her to sort out the clothes. Noneh was asking her to do more things like that, now that Zari was getting older and Jasmina was about to get married. There were a lot of clothes to take off the line, and she had to be sure she folded them properly, as well. This meant she was out in the back for a very long time, and while she was out there, she heard people talking.

She knew it was Mrs Jamaica right away. Mrs Jamaica's back door was open; Zari could just see the tip of it over the top of the fence. Also, she could hear that it was Mrs Jamaica's voice. She must be sitting in the kitchen, having a chat with someone, as usual. The someone this time was Jasmina. There was nothing strange in that. Jasmina didn't visit the Jamaicas as much as Zari did, but she did go over there from time to time, and she liked them well enough. Zari had heard her tell Noneh, about an hour ago, that she would just be next door at the Jamaica's, so not to wonder about her.

Everything about the situation was so usual that there was no reason for Zari to eavesdrop. But taking washing off the line is a bit boring, and there was nothing else to listen to, and gradually Zari realised she had been listening to their conversation for a long time. She had been listening without really paying attention to it, just like she did at school sometimes, when the teacher was going on and on about something Zari didn't really care about. Sometimes the teacher caught her doing this, but if he asked her what he had just said, Zari could usually tell him if she thought hard enough, even though she didn't know she had heard. Now, Zari realised her sister had just said, "But it's so *hard!*"

There was nothing very exciting about that, either. Jasmina did well in her studies at the college, but she always said they were difficult, even though no one really believed her. Probably she was just complaining to Mrs Jamaica about an exam she had to revise for. Only it was summer holidays. There were no exams to revise for. Zari listened to hear what Mrs Jamaica would say next, to see if she could figure out what it was Jasmina thought was so hard.

What Mrs Jamaica said was, "He said it would be hard, darling." That wasn't much help.

Jasmina sighed, which wasn't much help either, but then she said, "I know, but I thought—I don't know. I thought he'd help a little more, so it wouldn't *seem* hard."

Mrs Jamaica laughed. "No one helped him much, did they? That was part of the point of his coming here—to see what it felt like to be us. That way no one could say it wasn't fair and he just didn't understand and all that, remember? And now we suffer in the tiniest way for him, but it'll all come right in the end."

"But why can't it come right, right now?"

"Well, some of it might, too, love. But that's what you have to try. What did you mean when you promised yourself to him six months ago?"

Zari stopped taking the clothes off the line altogether. Jasmina had promised herself to someone? But she was engaged to Sokol—and Zari was fairly certain Mrs Jamaica wasn't talking about him. Was that what was hard? Maybe Jasmina had promised herself to someone else, and didn't know how to tell Noneh and Boba. That would be hard. Maybe she had met a Christian at college and promised herself to him. Maybe that's what all those questions about someone becoming a Christian had been about. That would be even harder. Zari was starting to get a horrible feeling in her stomach, but it made her want to keep listening to find out if she was right.

Only suddenly Noneh came out and said, rather shortly, "Zarifeh! What on earth are you doing, daydreaming out here, and wrinkling all the washing!" Zari stood up and realised she had been sitting on the pile of clean clothes she was meant to be bringing inside.

"Sorry, Noneh, but—" she began. She had been about to say, "but Jasmina's over at Mrs Jamaica's, talking about how she promised herself to someone who isn't Sokol." Only she couldn't quite say it. A year ago, she would have blabbed the whole thing right away—to Ekrem at least, and he would have blabbed it to the rest. But she had had so many secrets lately, ever since she and Sophie had stopped being friends, that she was starting to think it wasn't always necessary to tell everyone everything. Especially when it was so complicated. What would happen to her family if they found out Jasmina had a secret boyfriend? What would happen if they found out Mrs Jamaica was helping her? Zari picked up the wrinkled washing and carried it into the house. She was starting to feel angry at Mrs. Jamaica again. What right did she have to interfere with Zari's family like this? The only good thing Zari could think of that might come out of this whole mess would be if Sokol was willing to wait for her to grow up, and marry her instead.

She wanted to listen to the rest of the conversation, but when she went back outside, she noticed that the Jamaicas' back door was closed. They must have heard Noneh talking to her. Zari wondered if they guessed she had been listening. What would she do when she saw Jasmina? She would have to pretend she had not heard a thing. In the meantime, she was going out front.

The boys were playing at the other end of the street, but Zari did not feel like playing with them today. Apart from their yells, and an occasional out of control kick which sent the ball sailing down toward Zari's end of the street, endangering all the car windscreens, no one else was about and everything was quiet. Zari leaned against the front gate and thought what to do. She looked up the road to where Sophie's mother still lived, without Sophie. Just after the summer holidays began, Sophie had gone to live with her father in Southampton. Zari knew this because there had been talk about it at school before it happened. She felt a little sorry that she and Sophie had never made up, but since they hadn't, it was probably best that they weren't living over the road from each other any more.

The house next to Sophie's mother's had a sort of prickly-bumpy front and had been painted a colour somewhere between pale pink and pale orange. The windows were new—double-glazed ones which were supposed to keep everything warmer in winter, and maybe cooler in summer, though Zari couldn't understand how "double" of anything could make anyone cooler. Above the front door was a shiny, bright green sticker with words from the Qur'an written on it. Zari couldn't read them, because she couldn't read

Arabic, but she could recognise Arabic when she saw it, and anyway, she knew the people in that house were Muslim. It was Sajda's house. With Sophie gone, Sajda probably didn't have anyone to play with either.

There was no car parked in front of her house, which Zari was pretty certain meant that Sajda's mother was home and Sajda's father was still at work. At least, that's what it meant when the car was away in the daytime at Zari's house. She took a step forward. What would Sajda say if she knocked for her? Would she come out and play, or would she treat Zari the way Zari had first treated her? Zari didn't really want to find out, but she also didn't want to spend the rest of the afternoon by herself. She took a deep breath and crossed the street.

A teenage boy answered the door. Zari had seen him before in the street, but she didn't think he was Sajda's brother. Maybe a cousin. He looked at her without much interest. "Yeah?" he asked.

"Is Sajda home?" Zari asked. Her voice was shaking, which surprised her. It wasn't like she was going to cry or anything. And there was no point in being nervous. Either Sajda was home or she wasn't. And if she was home she would either come out, which would mean that she was nice, and maybe worth playing with after all, or she wouldn't come out, which would mean that she was nasty, just as Zari had always thought.

"Yeah," said the boy again, not moving or changing the bored expression on his face.

"Can she come out?" asked Zari.

The boy turned his head just a little bit, in the direction of the stairs behind him. "Sajda!" he yelled, in a voice that made Zari want to cover her ears, but she didn't.

A pair of bare feet and trousered legs appeared at the top of the stairs. The hallway was dark and Zari was too far back from the door to see the person's head.

"Yeah?" asked a voice that must have belonged to the same person as the legs.

Zari crouched down until she could see Sajda's face. "Hiya, Sajda," she said, very quietly. She hoped Sajda could hear her. She didn't seem able to make her voice any louder. "I was wondering if you would come out and play with me."

There was a very long silence, until the teenage boy in the doorway snapped something at Sajda in Urdu. She replied back to him in the same language, and the boy turned to Zari. "She said she'll think about it," he said. And then, for the first time he really looked at her and winked. "I'll help her think!" he whispered, and closed the door. Zari stood facing the closed door for what felt like a long time, but probably really wasn't. Then she turned and went back across the street.

She climbed up on the wall in front of their house and drew faces in the dust on the top of it, with her finger. She wanted to make smiling faces, but all of the smiles came out as nearly straight lines, for some reason. She jumped back off the wall, and almost went to knock at

Mrs Jamaica's until she remembered that Jasmina was over there, having a top-secret conversation which would almost certainly stop if Zari showed up. Maybe the back door was open again and she could hear something that way. It wouldn't hurt to find out. She knocked on the door of her own house—Boba said she was still too young to keep track of a key—and Noneh let her in.

"It's boring, Noneh," Zari groaned. "I wish Sophie were here!" Of course, if Sophie had been there, they probably still wouldn't be speaking to each other, but Noneh didn't need to know that. "I'm going to sit in the back garden and get a tan." Lavdita was always trying to get a tan. She thought it was very American and, since she firmly believed everything American was better than anything British, tans, to her, were very important. Zari thought tanning might be important to British people too, but it would be very hard for any of them to get one, since it rained so often. But it was sunny now. Before Noneh could object, Zari whipped a towel out of the pile of clean washing and flung it onto the grass in the back garden. She flung herself on top of it. Noneh started to say something, but gave up and sighed. Zari lay on her stomach with her eyes closed and felt the sunlight resting warmly on her arms and legs. It was nice.

There were no voices coming over the garden fence. Mrs Jamaica must have left the door closed. Zari had forgotten to check before she lay down. But she was too comfortable to move now. The bees buzzed overhead in the bushes, but Zari was not afraid of them. She thought maybe that was what the sunlight sounded like—the bee-sound and the warm light always seemed to go together. After a few minutes, she fell asleep.

Noneh was calling her, and when she called back, Noneh couldn't hear her—and then she woke up and realised that Noneh really was calling her, but she sounded far away. Zari jumped up, still half-asleep, with towel-marks on her face. Noneh was in the front hallway, with the door open. Someone was standing in the doorway, but with the light behind the person, and the sleep still in Zari's head, Zari couldn't tell who it was.

"Do you know this girl?" Noneh was asking in Albanian.

"Yes," said Zari after a few more blinks, when she could see better. "It's Sajda. She's in my class and lives just over the road. Didn't you know that?"

"She wants you to play with her," Noneh said. "Do you play with this girl?"

Zari paused a moment. She thought about Sajda making her wait while she thought about it. Zari didn't think that had been very nice. But she hadn't been very nice to Sajda first. And if she was not nice again now, then Sajda would keep being not nice... It would never end, they would never play with each other, and in the meantime, the rest of the summer holidays would be really dull. "Yes," said Zari. "I play with her." It wasn't

Summer Holidays

true of course; Zari and Sajda had never played with each other in their lives—except in P.E., when they had to and it didn't count. But if Zari went out and played with Sajda now, it would be true.

"Hiya Sajda," she said in English. She didn't feel nervous any more. "What do you want to play?"

113

# Eavesdropping

*G*emma wasn't fooled. "You don't play with Sajda," she said when Zari told her what she'd been doing at the weekend.

"I do now," Zari retorted. After that, Zari and Sajda played together during the day, and in the afternoons, when Gemma came back from riding horses, Sajda and Zari would troop over to her street and play some more. When a few weeks of this had gone by, Boba noticed.

"My Zarifeh's happy again," he said with satisfaction. Zari didn't realise she had seemed unhappy and said so.

"It's your eyes," he said. "Your eyes are just like your mother's, and I can always see in them if you're happy or not."

Zari had never thought about this, but she thought about it now. Boba was probably right about Noneh at least—except her eyes always looked sad. No, not always. Not when she was planning for Jasmina's wedding. Zari thought that was another good reason not to say anything about the conversation she had heard Jasmina having with Mrs Jamaica those weeks before.

"You don't limp any more, either," Ekrem called from the sitting room, were he was watching television instead of eating dinner. "You must be happy."

"You girls are good friends, aren't you?" Boba asked, not commenting on Zari's limping.

"Yeah," said Zari, popping a piece of bread into her mouth.

"How would you three like to go to the park together?"

Zari stirred her soup. "Agron's never home to take us any more, Boba," she whined.

"Without Agron," Boba said.

Zari stared at him, but she didn't get to say anything because Ekrem, who was still eavesdropping over his television programme, let out a howl and came rushing into the dining room, pouncing on his father's neck. "What about me?" he asked. "Can I go to the park without Agron, too?"

"I was talking to Zarifeh," Boba said, but Zari noticed that his eyes were smiling. She smiled, too—only it was probably more of a smirk. She didn't usually get special privileges before Ekrem.

"Zarifeh's got two good friends now," Boba continued.

"And the park's not far. If you three stay in the playground, my girl, and come back before it begins to get dark, you have my permission to go."

Zari let out a whoop that was louder than Ekrem's, and Ekrem got down on his knees on the floor next to Boba. "Me, too, Boba?" he begged. "Me, too?" He made his eyes look so big and innocent that Zari burst out laughing. Noneh got up suddenly and disappeared into the kitchen. She had been very quiet during this whole conversation, and hadn't smiled once. Zari imagined her eyes were not looking all that happy right now. She probably still thought it wasn't safe for Zari to go to the park even with her two friends.

Boba put on a stern face, too, and said to Ekrem, "Maybe—when someone starts eating Albanian dinner which his mother cooked for him, instead of buying chips round the corner with his friends, then maybe he and those friends will also have permission to go to the park on their own."

"Hah!" said Zari.

Ekrem jumped into the chair next to Noneh's empty one so fast that he almost knocked it over. Then he ripped an enormous chunk out of the loaf of bread and began munching on it.

"But Zarifeh," Boba said, turning back to his daughter, "you still can't go there alone. It has to be all three of you."

"Hah!" said Ekrem.

Zari slumped down in her chair. Gemma's parents might let them go, but she knew as well as Ekrem that the chances of Sajda's family letting her go to the park without an adult were almost non-existent.

Next day no one answered the door at Sajda's when Zari knocked, and Gemma was, as usual, gone for the morning. Zari skipped back across the street and knocked at Mrs Jamaica's instead. She hadn't seen Mrs Jamaica in ages, and she had a lot to tell her.

"Guess what, Mrs Jamaica?" she asked when the door opened.

"What, darling?" Mrs Jamaica chuckled, letting her in.

"I'm playing with Sajda now!"

"You are?" asked Mrs Jamaica, only she didn't sound as surprised as Zari thought she would.

"Oh—you probably saw us playing out your window, didn't you, Mrs Jamaica? Well, Boba said we can all go to the park together by ourselves now!"

"Together by yourselves, eh?" Mr Jamaica asked from the sitting room. Zari was startled. She hadn't expected him to be home. Ever since she had had traditional English Sunday dinner with the Jamaicas, she felt more comfortable with Mr Jamaica, but she still wasn't certain how she felt about telling all her secrets when he was around.

"I mean—oh, Mr Jamaica, *you* know what I mean!" she huffed.

118

"Of course he does, love," Mrs Jamaica assured her, with a note in her voice that sounded like it was telling Mr Jamaica to stop being so ridiculous. "Come on back to the kitchen with me and we'll talk where *he* can't be awkward." She put her head through the sitting room doorway and smiled sweetly, and then took it back out and Zari followed her to the kitchen.

Today Mrs Jamaica was not baking, which was surprising, but she had some biscuits left from the day before, and she put some out on a plate and made some tea while Zari sat and watched her. "I'm so glad you're playing with Sajda now, sweetheart," Mrs Jamaica said with her back to her. "Aren't you?"

"Yes," sighed Zari, "You were right, Mrs Jamaica. How come you're always right?"

"There's no way on earth I'm always right, child!" Mrs Jamaica turned around with the plate of biscuits. "Just ask Mr Jamaica. He'd be gladder than most to tell you. But I have been around a bit, and I've seen friendships end and friendships begin and friendships carry on, too, and I guess I know something about it."

That reminded Zari of something. "You're *not* always right," she said. "It's true. You're helping my sister when she promised herself to a Christian who isn't even Sokol, when Sokol is the one she's meant to get married to."

Mrs Jamaica, who had been smiling, suddenly looked very serious. "Who told you that, child?"

"I—no one—I..." Zari stopped. She had just tricked

119

herself into confessing that she had heard something she probably shouldn't have. Finally she took a deep breath and said, "I heard you talking to her, Mrs Jamaica. One day I was taking the washing down and your back door was open and I heard you talking."

"What exactly did you hear?" Mrs Jamaica asked.

Zari thought this was making Mrs Jamaica sound very guilty indeed, and so probably her guesses were exactly right, so she told Mrs Jamaica just what she had heard and what she had thought.

"Now that," said Mrs Jamaica when Zari had finished, "is a good reason for a person not to eavesdrop. I can see why you thought what you did, from what you heard, but you didn't hear the whole conversation, did you?"

"No," said Zari. She was starting to feel bad again, and wondered yet again why she kept going to Mrs Jamaica's if she was always going to tell her that she was doing something wrong.

"And if you didn't hear the whole conversation, you mostly likely weren't meant to. Privacy can be important, love, and I think you need to learn to respect that. But the other reason eavesdropping is a bad idea is that it usually leaves us without the whole picture, and we start thinking things that aren't true."

Zari was quiet. She thought about other times she had eavesdropped. She had listened when her mother and Zahe had begun arranging for Jasmina and Sokol to marry, and she had been right about that. Ekrem had eavesdropped last night and known exactly that Boba was giving her permission to go to the park, and not him. Maybe sometimes she might be wrong, but most of the time, listening to other people's conversations was useful, and besides that, all the ones she ever listened to had something to do with her or with people that she cared about.

"Listen, Mrs Jamaica," she said. "We're Albanians in my family. We don't have secrets from each other. If you're helping Jasmina have a boyfriend, it's my business because she's my sister. When I heard you talking to her, that wasn't wrong." She felt herself turn red as soon as she finished talking. Partly it was because they really did have secrets in their family—they just didn't seem to last very long. Partly it was because she thought she sounded very grown up just then, when she said that. But mostly it was because she could not believe she had told off Mrs Jamaica.

Mrs Jamaica, on the other hand, did not look as if she knew she had been told off. "Zari," she laughed, "I think your family has fewer secrets than they might just because you make it your business to listen to all of them. But honey, Jasmina doesn't have a boyfriend, and I'm not helping her to have one. And that's really why I'm telling you not to listen to conversations that aren't yours—because you'll start getting the wrong ideas. And one day you may hear something you wish you hadn't heard."

Zari looked into her tea and sipped out of it. "Well something's going on," she said, pouting. "You weren't just talking about nothing in here, were you?" Mrs Jamaica didn't say anything. Zari looked up at her. "Were you, Mrs Jamaica?"

"You're a clever girl, Zari," Mrs Jamaica said. "Not always right, but clever. Yes, something is going on, but like I told you once before, it's not something I can talk to you about. It isn't my place, because it isn't 'going on' with me. If you really want to know, you'll have to ask your sister. But take my advice and, if she doesn't tell you, just leave her be. She's having a hard enough time as it is."

Zari ate a biscuit. When she had finished it, she carefully wiped all the crumbs of it into her hand. Then she brushed them into her tea. "All right, Mrs Jamaica," she said.

"What are you and Sajda playing these days?" Mrs Jamaica asked, and as they finished their tea and biscuits, Zari told her. "One thing, Mrs Jamaica," she said as she got ready to leave, "Boba said we can only go to the park together if it's all three of us. But Sajda's father isn't going to let her go. He'll tell her a grown-up has to go, too, and none of her grown-ups will go."

"How do you know?" Mrs Jamaica asked.

"I just know," said Zari. "So Mrs Jamaica, if you're not baking, like you weren't today, could you take us to the park sometimes?"

Mrs Jamaica thought for a minute. "I don't see why not," she said at last. "Might do me good, in fact. Mr Jamaica's always saying I need to go out."

"Thank you, Mrs Jamaica!" Zari exclaimed, jumping up and giving her a big hug. "See you next time!"

"Bye, love," said Mrs Jamaica, seeing her out the door. "See you next time."

After supper, Zari stomped upstairs to find Jasmina. She was sitting on her bed in their room, leaning against the wall and staring over Zari's bed and out the window. Zari didn't think she was actually looking at anything out there. She jumped when Zari came in and started talking to her. "What's wrong, Jasmina?"

"What do you mean?" she asked, but she looked nervous.

"You're acting strange," said Zari. She didn't want to talk about her chat with Mrs Jamaica that afternoon until she had to, because if she did, she would have to tell Jasmina she had overheard one of her conversations. Thinking about it now, she decided if Mrs Jamaica had been unhappy with her about that, Jasmina would be even less pleased.

"What do you mean?" Jasmina asked again.

"You're quiet, and you don't eat, and right now you're sitting and looking out the window at nothing."

Jasmina laughed. "I was just thinking. I'm allowed to think, aren't I?"

"Come on!" Zari whined. Then she had an idea. "Look,"

she said, "I'm really really sorry, but a couple of weeks ago I heard you talking to Mrs Jamaica. I know I shouldn't have listened, and I'm really sorry, but anyway, I know there's something going on, and—since I told you about what I did wrong, can you tell me about yours?"

Zari thought Jasmina looked as if at any moment she would laugh, cry, or hit her, so while she was deciding, Zari said, "I haven't told Noneh or Boba."

Jasmina relaxed then, and slumped back down against the wall. "Zari," she said, "I can't tell you. I want to tell you—I'm just not ready. But I will tell you, all right? I promise. Only please, promise *me* that you won't tell Noneh and Boba."

It occurred to Zari that she could threaten to tell them the little bit she knew unless Jasmina told her the whole secret. But then it also occurred to her that if she did, probably Mrs Jamaica would find out about it somehow and make her feel bad about it the next time she saw her. Besides, Jasmina was looking so frightened and unhappy just now. Tricking her into telling a secret would only make whatever it was worse, and that might just make Zari feel worse, too. No secret was worth all that. "I promise," she said.

The phone rang. Zari and Jasmina both heard Ekrem and Agron, who still wrestled over the phone for old times' sake, thumping around at the bottom of the stairs, each one trying to get to it first. There was a pause while the phone stopped ringing as Agron, who usually won, answered it and everyone in the house, both upstairs and down, tried to guess who was calling.

"*Allo*?" said Agron.

There was another moment of silence. Then, "Jasmina!" he bellowed up the stairs.

Jasmina jumped off the bed and went into the hallway. "Noneh, may I use the phone in your room?" she called down. Zari could hear Noneh start to say something, but Boba answered over her instead. "Yes, but don't be too long! We're waiting for Zahe to phone." Jasmina went into her parents' room and shut the door behind her.

"*Allo*?" Jasmina's voice through the door was very quiet, but Zari could just hear it. She wondered how much it was possible to hear through a door, if the person spoke very quietly. Sometimes she could hear Muqeem's parents arguing through the wall that his house shared with hers. A wall was surely thicker than a door. Maybe she could investigate how much you could hear through a wall compared to a door for science class, when school started up in two weeks. She would ask her new teacher about it. In the meantime, it might be a good idea to start on this investigation now. It could take a long time, because of course the results would be different depending on how loud or soft people's voices were. Somewhere in the back of her mind she almost remembered Mrs Jamaica's warning against eavesdropping, but she wasn't really eavesdropping, was she? She was doing a science investigation.

The first thing she heard was Jasmina saying, "Hang up, Agron!" Then, not through the door at all, but up the stairs, she heard her two brothers giggling, and the loud clunk of the receiver as they threw it clumsily back into the cradle of the downstairs phone. They were the ones who had really been eavesdropping. Zari sat quietly in the dim hallway with her shoulder and ear against the door while Jasmina, on the other side of it, said to whoever was on the phone, "I'm almost ready to tell them."

There was a moment of quiet. Zari wished she could hear the person on the phone through the door, too, but that would be a pointless investigation. She wouldn't be able to hear them even if she was in the same room as her sister—unless, of course, she was the one talking on the phone.

Now Jasmina was saying, "I know, but I thought about what Mrs Jamaica said, and she's right." After the next pause she went on, "No, she didn't tell me what I have to do. She said there are never any easy answers, but she gave me two options as she sees them... No, that's what she called them... She said the Bible says not to join in partnership with unbelievers and she thinks that means marriage, so I could just tell them I'm not going to marry him..."

Zari stiffened. The *Bible*? Jasmina must have meant the Qur'an. But Zari didn't think Jasmina read the Qur'an, and she knew Mrs Jamaica didn't. And then there was this business about her not marrying someone.

Now she *must* be talking about Sokol. Zari had known all this had something to do with Jasmina's marriage. Or non-marriage, as it was beginning to sound. But Sokol wasn't an unbeliever. He was a Muslim. Muslims were *the* believers. What could Jasmina be thinking? Zari kept listening.

"...or," Jasmina went on, "I could just keep quiet about the whole thing and marry him, if I really think that's best, because it also says to honour my father and mother, and if I married him to honour them, and then tried to be the best wife I can be, that would be okay, too. Only she said that eventually it would come out that I was a Christian, and it would be better if I told them. She said Jesus said if we are ashamed of him, his Father in Heaven would be ashamed of us. I don't want to be ashamed of Him any more, and I don't want Him to be ashamed of me..."

Zari stopped listening. She couldn't listen any more if she had wanted to, and she had stopped wanting to. It was as if her thoughts had frozen, her eardrums had frozen, she herself had frozen. She could not move for a very long time. She leaned stiffly against the door while Jasmina kept talking on the other side of it, but all Zari could hear was her saying, "It would come out that I was a Christian..."

After what seemed like a very long time, she got up quietly and tiptoed to her bedroom. She turned off the light, got undressed and pulled on the old white T-shirt in which she slept. Then she lay on her bed and stared blankly at the dark in the direction of the ceiling. Mrs Jamaica had been right again. Sometimes eavesdropping was just not worth it. You might hear something you wished you hadn't. Everything made sense now. And everything was more confusing than ever.

# The Park

*M*rs Jamaica came out her front door with Jasmina, "I thought that you girls might like to go to the park," she smiled.

It was only the next day, but to Zari it felt like it had been weeks. She had gone outside and played with Sajda as usual, but she felt like a robot. Gemma had come over and she still felt like a robot. She had been so distracted that she hadn't even been able to ask her friends about going to the park herself. It didn't seem very important or exciting any more. But when Mrs Jamaica asked, she shrugged and said, "I don't mind."

"Yes! Let's go to the park!" said Gemma, who rarely had to ask her parents for permission to do anything. Sajda looked doubtful for a moment and then said, "Just wait here, I'll ask my mum." She dashed off and disappeared into the house. Zari leaned against the front wall, crossed her arms over her chest, and sank her head down over them so she could almost feel her chin on her collar-bone. She thought Mrs Jamaica would ask her what was wrong, but she didn't. Sajda and Gemma had given up asking her what was wrong earlier, because she wouldn't tell them. She wouldn't tell Mrs Jamaica either, if she asked, but of course Mrs Jamaica would know exactly what was wrong.

Zari glanced up as Jasmina passed her and went into their own house. Jasmina's face was whiter than usual, and her lips were pressed shut, but her eyes were bright with something which looked more like excitement than fear. Jasmina glanced at Zari, too, as she went past. She did something with her mouth that Zari supposed was meant to be a smile, though it didn't look much like one, with her lips clamped together that tightly. Zari grimaced back at her, unsympathetically, and then put her chin back against her collar-bone.

Sajda had come back out by this time, and she was skipping, which looked like good news. Mrs Jamaica certainly took it that way. "Excellent!" she said, as if completely unaware that anything was wrong. "Come along then." She walked down to the end of the street, with Gemma and Sajda walking happily on either side of her and chattering away to her. Zari plodded along behind them all, scuffing her feet.

She didn't exactly know what she was so upset about.

She liked Christians. Mrs Jamaica was one of the nicest people Zari knew, even though she did make her feel naughty sometimes when she didn't know she had been. Mr Jamaica made her laugh. The teacher who did the Christian religious assemblies at school admitted in front of everyone once that she loved Jesus, and she seemed nice enough, too. Besides all that, no one had ever actually answered Mrs Jamaica's question about what they would do if someone in their family became a Christian, so Zari had no actual proof that anyone would be upset about it. But Zari knew they would be, and the reason she knew was that *she* was upset about it. She just had to find out why.

"I get the baby swing!" Gemma called out as they reached the corner of the park. She raced ahead toward the swing-set. The baby swing was the one with the back to lean against and the bar across the front. It was really too small for girls who were almost nine years old, but last school term all of Zari's classmates had made it a tradition to compete with each other for that swing. No one could fit under the bar, but they could sit on top of it, or they could put their feet in the seat and swing standing up. Sajda tore after Gemma, ended up outrunning her, to her own surprise, and got the swing herself. Zari kept scuffing her feet.

"What's wrong with Zari?" Zari heard Mrs Jamaica ask the two shrieking girls. Gemma, not put off at all by Sajda's getting the favourite swing, had jumped into an ordinary swing next to her, and they were trying to see who could swing the highest.

"Don't know," said Gemma. "She's been like that all day."

"She wouldn't tell us anything," Sajda added.

Mrs Jamaica sat down on a bench. Zari sat down on one as far away from her as possible without going out of the playground, and sank her chin against her collar-bone again. It wasn't very comfortable, but it was the best way she could think of to show Mrs Jamaica she was angry, without throwing a temper tantrum.

Mrs Jamaica got up and sat on Zari's bench.

Zari turned around, putting her feet up on the bench next to her, with her back to Mrs Jamaica. This time she rested her chin on her knees.

No one said anything for a while. The sky was grey and it was quite cold, even though it was August. Zari thought it was the right kind of weather to be angry in. She thought the weather was angry, too—as if God were trying to show Jasmina that she shouldn't have changed religions like that. Only probably Jasmina didn't notice.

"Are you angry at me, honey?" Mrs Jamaica asked.

"God's angry, too," Zari said into her knees.

"Pardon?"

"God's angry, too," Zari repeated, very slowly and clearly, with her head up so that Mrs Jamaica could hear her properly.

"He is?"

"Yes."

"How do you know?"

"It's cold," Zari said. "And cloudy. That's how I feel inside, and I'm angry, and God makes the weather, so He must be angry, too."

Mrs Jamaica chuckled. "In that case, he must be angry at poor old England an awful lot. It's always cold and cloudy here!"

"It's because they're all Christians," said Zari, without thinking too much about it.

Mrs Jamaica was quiet for a long time. Zari couldn't tell if she agreed or disagreed or felt bad or what, but she wasn't going to turn around and look at her to find out. Finally Zari said, "Mrs Jamaica, why did you make Jasmina a Christian?"

Mrs Jamaica made a strange sound which reminded Zari of a sigh and a grunt at the same time. Then she said, "Lovely, I didn't make Jasmina into a Christian."

"But she's a Christian," Zari said, still accusing her.

"Yes."

"So who did, then?"

"Well," Mrs Jamaica said slowly, "*I* would say it was God. I'd say God's the only one who can help someone change their heart like that. But I guess you wouldn't say that, would you, since you think God's angry at the Christians? So, just so we can have an explanation that makes sense to both of us, I guess we could also say Jasmina made herself a Christian."

"What—she just woke up one day and said, 'I think I'll be a Christian now'?"

Mrs Jamaica laughed. "No, I don't really think it was like that, although I expect some people decide to belong to Jesus in just that way."

Zari got a funny feeling in her stomach when Mrs Jamaica said that. Somehow it sounded different when she brought Jesus into it. Zari still liked Jesus, even though she didn't like Jasmina becoming a Christian. "You said she was a Christian," said Zari. "You didn't say anything about Jesus."

"I have now," Mrs Jamaica chuckled. "And anyway, how could a person become a Christian and leave Jesus out of it? Don't you remember when I told you how I changed my faith? I wasn't really a Christian until I started to try to live like Jesus, and with Jesus—even though I thought I was before."

Zari remembered. She just didn't understand it. "Well, I don't want Jasmina to be a Christian," she said stubbornly. "I want her to be a Muslim like us. She's *my* sister. She's Albanian."

"She'll always be your sister," said Mrs Jamaica. "And she won't stop being Albanian, either. Jesus is for everybody, honey, from every country—not just some. He's the Son of God, and God's the God of the whole world."

That made Zari's stomach feel funny, too, just like it had the first time Mrs Jamaica had said something like that. She remembered that Christians were all going to be destroyed by Allah at the end of the world because they believed Jesus was God. Zari bit her lip. If Jasmina was a Christian, she must believe that Jesus was God, too. And if she believed that, she was going to go to Hell.

Zari put her face on her knees so Mrs Jamaica couldn't see, and didn't say anything. But she couldn't keep her shoulders from shaking. Mrs Jamaica put her hand on them, gently. "Zari, love," she said, sounding very worried and kind all of a sudden, "are you all right?"

"I don't want Jasmina to be a Christian," Zari sobbed. "I don't want her to go to Hell!" She thought Mrs Jamaica would try to convince her that Jasmina wasn't going to go to Hell, but Mrs Jamaica didn't. She just sat there with her hand on Zari's shoulder, until Zari turned around and put her head on her lap, still crying softly. It seemed a bit crazy to her, even then, to be crying and comforted on the lap of a person she was angry at. But somehow Zari knew at that moment that even if Mrs Jamaica didn't agree with her about everything, at least she understood. Mrs Jamaica moved her hand from Zari's shoulder to her hair, smoothing it and smoothing it until at last Zari almost forgot what she had been crying about, and stopped. They sat there for another long time, completely silently, while Sajda and Gemma, and a few other children who had come to the park in the meantime, shouted and whooped in the background. Just as Zari was about to fall asleep, Mrs Jamaica moved and said, "Come along, honey. We need to get you home."

# The Announcement

*P*robably Mrs Jamaica had meant for Zari to be at the park with her when the news broke. Probably she had thought that would make things easier. But the house was still all quiet when they returned home, and when Jasmina, still white-faced and bright-eyed, answered the door, both Mrs Jamaica and Zari could see she hadn't told anyone anything. "I couldn't," she whispered to Mrs Jamaica over Zari's head before she shut the door. "I needed Zari here, too. What if I can only say it once?"

Zari looked back at Mrs Jamaica. Mrs Jamaica nodded. "I hadn't thought of that," she admitted. "I'll pray for you girls." Zari wondered if God would hear Mrs Jamaica's prayers after all this, and if he did, what he would do about them.

Jasmina closed the door and Zari took her shoes off. Neither sister said anything. After Zari's shoes were off, Jasmina turned and went to the dining room table and sat down. Zari followed. Dinner was laid out already, and Boba, Noneh, and the boys were eating it. Agron and Ekrem were making a lot of noise and obviously didn't realise that there was anything wrong at all.

Then Boba said, "My girls are quiet tonight."

It was a question, even though it didn't sound like one. Zari looked at the piece of bread in her hand and said nothing. Jasmina didn't answer the question, either. She giggled, and it sounded so nervous and strange that even Agron looked at her with curiosity, but no one said anything. The boys went back to their dinner. Noneh stared at Jasmina for the rest of the meal. Agron got up finally and said, "I'm going out."

"Wait!" Jasmina cried suddenly, reaching out her hand and holding on to Agron's arm. "Please, don't go anywhere. At least not yet. Please. I have to say something."

Agron wasn't one to wait for anyone if he wanted to do something. But Jasmina was behaving so oddly that he stopped.

Now everyone was staring at her. Zari noticed her sister had tears in her eyes already. She thought it was bad news if Jasmina was already crying and hadn't even said anything yet.

"Well then," said Boba, after a pause. "Say it."

138

"Could we go into the sitting room?" Jasmina asked in a small voice.

They all marched into the sitting room. It was very unnatural. No one in Zari's family ever announced that they should go into the sitting room. They just ended up there eventually, one way or another. Zari didn't think this was going very well at all. Everyone sat down in a chair or on the settee—even Noneh, who usually sat on the floor. It felt very formal and serious. Everyone looked at Jasmina again.

She blinked, cleared her throat, and finally said, "You're all going to say it was Mrs Jamaica's fault, but it wasn't; I didn't start going to see her until it had already happened."

No one had any idea what on earth she was talking about yet, except Zari. She thought probably their best guess was the one she had had at first: that Jasmina had a boyfriend who wasn't Sokol. Boba and Noneh were looking at Jasmina very hard.

"What happened?" asked Noneh. Her voice sounded hard like her eyes. Zari knew that meant she was afraid. Zari was afraid, too, and she knew what was coming. She tried to imagine how she would be feeling if she didn't know, but it made her too uncomfortable, so she stopped.

"I—" Jasmina began, and then she started again. "Some people at college all knew each other before they started taking courses there, and they would meet for

139

lunch most days. I got to know one of them; she was in my English class and she was from Italy. She was a really nice person and one day she asked if I would like to eat with them. They were all very kind." Jasmina paused. Then she took a deep breath, and said very quickly, as if all her words were one long word,

"They-were-studying-the-Bible-together-at-lunch-and-after-a-few-weeks-I-realised-it-was-true-and-so-I-decided-I-believe-in-Jesus."

Zari expected a shriek from her mother, and a yell from her father. Probably it would have happened just like that if Jasmina had said, "I decided to become a Christian." But she hadn't said that, and so now no one spoke or moved except Boba, and he spoke calmly. "You already believed in Jesus, didn't you?" he asked. "Everybody believes in Jesus." He didn't seem angry. It seemed as if he were trying to give Jasmina a way out—a way to make it sound as if she still believed the same as the rest of the family, a way to keep the family quiet and peaceful. Noneh, on the other hand, though still silent, was beginning to look as if someone had lit a fire under her and she was about to explode. But she waited until she heard how Jasmina would reply, first.

"I believed Jesus was a prophet before," Jasmina said. "But I didn't know anything about him then. Now I do, and I know that he could not have done the things he did and said the things he said if he were only a Prophet. It's impossible."

140

"Why?" asked Boba, who seemed genuinely to want to know.

"Because he himself claimed to be one with God, and that God was his Father. So either he was insane or lying, or he was telling the truth. But he can't be just a Prophet under any of those conditions." Jasmina had stopped looking as if she was about to cry. She had stopped sounding nervous. Her voice was still quiet, but clear and strong, as if the things she was saying were the things she was surest about in all the world. "He was too good to be lying or crazy, so he must have been telling the truth," she went on, "and I believe it. I believe that Jesus is God on earth and that when the people who hated him brought him to the cross, they really did kill him. But I also believe that he came back to life. I trust what the Bible says, which is that he died the death I deserved for all the bad things I have ever done, and that, since he came back to life, I will come back to life with him after I die, too."

Boba looked sceptical. He opened his mouth to ask another question, which looked as if it would be awkward and ironic, but before he could ask it, Noneh burst out, "What have you done?"

Everyone craned round to look at her. "Allah preserve us!" she cried, getting to her feet. "What have you done? You foolish, foolish girl—how could you?!" Usually Noneh was very quiet. She would sit in a corner and listen to what was happening and form her own opinions but never say a word. But once she was angry, she could shout for hours. Zari thought this might be one of those shouting times.

"How could I...?" Jasmina began, but Noneh interrupted her. She stood in front of Jasmina where she sat on the settee, and she shouted. She shouted that Jasmina was irresponsible and disrespectful of her family and her heritage and her upbringing. She yelled that Jasmina had given up all her chances of a respectable marriage, because Sokol would never marry her now, and she had ruined her family's reputation. How would they find good wives for Agron and Ekrem now? And no one would ever want Zarifeh after this disgrace.

Zari secretly thought that by the time she was ready to marry, everyone would have forgotten Jasmina so it wouldn't affect her chances in the slightest. She didn't bother to announce to Noneh just then that she might want to worry about Agron, who had been going out with an English girl for a year behind Noneh's back.

Noneh simply carried on yelling at Jasmina. She wailed that she herself must have done something terrible for Allah to punish her in this way with a rebellious daughter, one who even went so far as to commit *shirk*—the sin of making a human being equal to God. Finally, she began to absolutely scream. "And *this*," she screamed, "is what comes of leaving one's homeland. I knew we should never have come here—to this horrible, dirty, grey *Christian* place—this England!" She fell to her knees in the middle of the room. It seemed she had stopped shouting at Jasmina, and was either shouting at everybody all at once, or at nobody at all.

"Kosovo!" she cried, "At least there children know how to respect their parents. You don't have girls rejecting the faith. You don't have boys going off until all hours of the night to visit with girls who are not their people..."

Zari noticed that she and both her brothers and Jasmina jumped at that. None of them had realised Noneh knew about Agron's girlfriend. She hoped Agron wouldn't pound her later for tattling on him, because she hadn't.

"...And none of this mixing with Christians! In Kosovo we know who the Christians are—they're the Serbs, and everyone knows Albanians don't mix with Serbs. But now we are in England, and the Christians are different. That's what you say!" Noneh looked at Boba first, but then her eyes swung round the room so that everyone was included in her stare. "That's what you all say! But they're not! They're all the same! They're liars, and they divide up your family and kill the ones you love..." Suddenly she burst into tears, and couldn't say any more.

Zari looked around at the rest of the family. Ekrem sat as far back into the cushions of his chair as he could, and his face was white as a sheet. Agron, who was clearly trying to work out how Noneh had known about his girlfriend, was muttering what were probably curse-words under his breath and scowling. Jasmina's knees were pulled up in front of her on the settee, and she clutched them with her arms so that all Zari could see was her eyes and hair. Her eyes were streaming with tears. Boba sat with his fists clenched and a number of different expressions flitting across his face. She was so used to seeing him laughing that Zari couldn't tell if he were frightened or concerned or angry now, and if he were angry, she couldn't tell who he was angry at.

All she knew was that her family was a mess. So she got off the couch, knelt beside Noneh, and hugged her. She hugged her for a long time. Then she marched upstairs, got into her nightshirt, and went to bed.

# Making Noise

*S*chool started the next week. The leaves were starting to fall in big leafy puddles onto the pavements. When Zari looked up at the trees, she could just see the stubs of the branches which had been cut in the spring. Mostly, however, she didn't look up. If she did there was danger of falling, because the leaves under her feet were very slippery.

Sajda joined her as she walked to school. They met Gemma at the corner, and she hurried along with them. Ekrem and his friends were somewhere in the background. Zari, Gemma, and Sajda were moving to the upper half of the school this year, which meant they were old enough to walk to and from school without any of their parents. It also meant that Ekrem could no longer tease them for being "little children." But she and her friends knew that Ekrem and his friends would still keep their distance. Zari didn't mind. She didn't need to play football with the boys any longer.

"Are your parents still keeping your sister locked up?" asked Sajda.

"Yes," admitted Zari.

"They could get in trouble for that," said Gemma. "It's a good thing for them that nobody knows."

"*You* both know," said Zari, a little uncomfortably.

"Oh, but we'll never tell anyone," said Sajda.

"No, we won't tell," said Gemma. Then she turned to Sajda and said, "My parents said probably your parents wouldn't let you play with Zari any more, since her sister has become a Christian."

"They're not like that," said Sajda, looking a little annoyed. "They know it isn't Zari's fault."

Zari was relieved. She was pretty certain that Muqueem's parents would have made him stop playing with her and Ekrem, if they had still been friends, which they weren't. Zari put her arms around her friends' shoulders as the three of them entered the school yard.

At lunchtime, Gemma asked, "Will Mrs Jamaica take us to the park again, do you think?"

"No," Zari sighed. "I'm not allowed to see her any more. Noneh and Boba think she's going to try to make me a Christian, as well."

"My parents said that, too," Sajda admitted. "She's the one who converted your sister after all, isn't she?"

"No!" said Zari indignantly. "It was some friends of Jasmina's from college. Mrs Jamaica was just someone nearby to talk to, who would understand."

"That's what your sister says," Gemma said, darkly. "But some Christians just can't seem to shut up about their religion. They should just stop being arrogant and let people believe what they want to. That's what my mum says. We're Church of England, but we don't go around telling people what to believe all the time."

All three girls were quiet for a minute, thinking about this, and then Zari said, "Mrs Jamaica's Church of England, too, I think. But you aren't really a Christian, are you? Mrs Jamaica said..."

"Oh, do we have to keep talking about Mrs Jamaica?" Gemma spluttered, exasperated. "Let's talk about something else. Race you to that tree over there!" They all dashed off and Gemma won, which clearly made her feel better.

When school was over, they raced each other part of the way home, and after they got to Zari's street, they had races there. Being the fastest, Gemma won most of them. After she left, Zari and Sajda slumped, exhausted, against Sajda's front wall.

"We'll have to practice so we can beat her next time!" Sajda panted.

"I think that *was* practice," Zari groaned. "I don't think I want to practice ever again!" She started to say something else when a car pulled up in front of her house. It was Zahe. She was there with her husband, and Lavdita, and Sokol. Zari groaned quietly.

"What's wrong?" asked Sajda.

"Here comes the next bit of trouble for my sister," Zari said. "I think I have to go indoors. See you tomorrow, Sajda. If I live." She followed Lavdita into the house.

"Hiya, Zari!" said Lavdita. She sounded much too happy and friendly, Zari thought, for it to be true.

"Hello, Lavdita," said Zari warily. The grown-ups were taking their seats in the sitting room already. Noneh was bustling about in the kitchen making tea. Zari was quite certain that Noneh had not told Zahe exactly what had happened to Jasmina. Noneh had been hoping maybe Jasmina would change her mind after being shut up in the house for a few days. If Jasmina had been baptised as a Christian, everyone knew they would all have had to give up on her immediately. It would have meant that she was going through far more than a phase. Jasmina insisted that it wasn't a phase. But she had no baptism papers yet, and Noneh could hope. Zari thought that Noneh might have mentioned to Zahe that they were having a little trouble with Jasmina, without explaining exactly what. If Zahe knew what had happened, it could only be that Agron had told Lavdita's brother, which was even worse than Noneh explaining it herself.

"I'll make tea, Noneh," Zari said. "Lavdita can help me." She had never been bold enough before to suggest that Lavdita would help her do anything, but these were special circumstances. She heard Jasmina coming down the stairs. Then she heard Noneh snap something at her under her breath, and Jasmina went back up. Zari bit her lip. Were they not even going to let Jasmina explain?

She turned the tap on and filled the lower kettle while Lavdita put the tea leaves and more water in the smaller, upper one. Zari put the lower kettle on the cooker, turned on the gas, and lit it. Lavdita set her kettle into the hole on the top of the larger one and they waited for it to boil. Neither of them said anything. Zari got out a plate and put three kinds of biscuit on it. She could hear the grown-ups talking in the other room. Their voices had started off quiet and polite, but now they were beginning to sound a little more excited. Zari hoped Boba would come home soon. She thought that Zahe and her husband and Sokol would start telling Noneh off for being a bad mother and letting her children spend time with unsuitable people, or something, and Noneh would need someone on her side after a while.

Just as Zari finished thinking this, Boba came in the front door. He went straight to the sitting room. Zari put the tea glasses, sugar, and biscuits on one tray. Lavdita put the double kettle on another. Then they both marched to the sitting room as well.

Zahe had been in the middle of saying something, but when she saw Zari, she broke off and started cooing. "Oh, Zarifeh!" she cooed. "Come here, you poor girl."

Zari thought, if this whole thing were about Jasmina,

why was *she* a "poor girl"? But she put the tea things down and went to her, even though she didn't want to. Zahe took her hands and pulled her next to her on the settee, and then wrapped her arms around Zari's head and gave her a hug. Zari thought that maybe she was glad that Zahe and her family were about to have a fight with Noneh and Boba.

"Let the 'poor girl' go, then," said Sokol, with something of a laugh in his voice. "How do you expect her to breathe?"

Zari thought, as Zahe let go of her head, that the bad thing about Zahe and her family having a fight with Boba and Noneh was that she would never see Sokol again. She also thought, briefly, that it was truly ridiculous of Jasmina to give up someone like him in exchange for Jesus, who the Christians said had died, and who, at any rate, was invisible. Sokol was sitting in the chair next to the settee where Zahe, her husband, and now Zari, were sitting. Zari stayed where she was, just because it allowed her to be closer to him than she would have been if she had moved and sat on the floor.

"Maybe," said Zahe to Boba and Noneh, as if she was finishing the thing she had been saying before Zari came in, "we should have Jasmina come down here after all. I'm quite curious to hear how all this has happened. And I have a feeling we might be able to convince her to change her mind." Zari didn't think so, but Zahe wasn't talking to her.

Noneh got up and went to fetch Jasmina. When Jasmina came down, she looked frightened but determined. She stood in the doorway and looked at everyone. "Sit down, darling," said Zahe, even though there were no chairs left. Zari wondered who had made Zahe the boss at this meeting. Sokol stood up and motioned for Jasmina to have his chair. Jasmina looked startled by this, but she took the chair. Sokol sat on the floor next to Boba.

"So," said Zahe, when no one else seemed about to say anything, "what's this we hear about you Jasmina? Is it true you have become a Christian?"

"Yes," said Jasmina simply.

"Can you tell us *why*?" Zahe asked.

Jasmina began to talk about Jesus and everything she thought he had done for her. Zari wondered how Jasmina could be so sure, even if Jesus really had done all those things, that it had been for *her*. She would have to ask her when all of these other people weren't here any more.

In the meantime, Zahe had interrupted. "I didn't ask you to tell me about Jesus—I wanted to know what was the reason you decided to become a Christian."

Jasmina looked puzzled. Zari felt puzzled. Even she thought that Jasmina had been answering the question. Jasmina said, "But that's why. Jesus is why."

Zahe sighed. Her sigh sounded as if she thought she were a very patient woman trying to get a confession out

151

of a very stubborn child. Zari wondered why no one else was saying anything. She thought that even if Noneh and Boba were still angry with Jasmina themselves, they should be defending her. She was their daughter, after all, and Zahe was just...annoying.

Zahe said, "I know you had some friends at college. They convinced you, didn't they?"

"They introduced me," corrected Jasmina. "Jesus convinced me."

Zahe said coldly, "Stop hiding what we all know is the truth—one of those friends of yours is your secret boyfriend."

Zari could tell Jasmina was getting angry, because she suddenly became sarcastic, and Jasmina was almost never sarcastic. She said, "Oh, really? Which one was he? Please tell me, because I hadn't noticed, myself."

Zahe looked offended, and Noneh made an angry sound at Jasmina. "You see?" said Zahe, looking around the two families. "She doesn't answer directly. It must be true."

"I apologise for the disrespect," Jasmina said, but Zari could hear in the back of her voice that she was still angry. "But it is not true that I have or ever have had a boyfriend."

"If we were in Kosovo," Zahe muttered, "you would never talk to me as you have just been doing." Zari opened her mouth to defend her sister and then shut it again, because Zahe was still talking. "If it's true what you say—that you never had a boyfriend," she was saying, more loudly, "perhaps you might want to reconsider your decision. You want to marry a Kosovar—other men will not treat you properly, and look," she indicated Sokol, who was still sitting on the floor, "here is a very good man for you, if you will only consent to be a Muslim again. It is impossible that you will get a better offer."

"I will not reconsider," Jasmina said, but when Zari turned her head to look at her, she saw that her sister was looking down, and her voice had gotten quieter.

Suddenly someone else spoke. It was Sokol. "She doesn't need to reconsider, Zahe," he said. "I will marry her anyway."

The room got very quiet. Everyone looked at Sokol. Then everyone looked at Jasmina. Finally Jasmina said, as if it were the hardest thing she had ever had to say, "I'm sorry. I cannot marry you. I can only marry someone who believes the same thing about Jesus that I do."

After that the room got very noisy. Noneh and Boba started shouting about their foolish, stupid, stubborn daughter and what was she thinking. Zahe began accusing Jasmina of not being a true Kosovar. Sokol started pleading with her to consider him anyway, and then when that didn't work, he disappointed Zari by making fun of Jasmina's beliefs instead. He teased her and asked how she could be so cold as to choose a religion over love. Jasmina said, "Choosing Jesus is love," but she said it very quietly, and probably only Zari heard it.

Zari listened to all this noise for a little while, but the more she listened, the angrier she got. She knew that just the week before she had been very angry at Jasmina herself. But so many people were angry with Jasmina now, and it just didn't seem fair. Jasmina had always been nicer than any of them, and even now she was only doing what she thought was right. Zari got angrier and angrier as she listened, until all of a sudden she found herself jumping up from the settee and yelling, "STOP!"

Everyone stopped. They all looked very surprised. Zari was surprised, too, but now that they had stopped, it was her turn to make noise. "What do you all think you're doing?" she shouted. "Why are you all being so selfish? What about Jasmina?" No one answered. She turned to Sokol. "You!" she said. "I liked you. You're handsome and all that and if I were older I would want to marry you myself, but it's no wonder my sister turned you down; she's clever. You don't believe in Jesus the way she does, just like she said. You act all nice until she turns you down and then you make fun of her for her beliefs. That's what you're really like, and why should she spend her life putting up with that?"

"And the rest of you!" Zari could hardly believe she was talking like this. It reminded her of the time when she told off the lorry driver who had brought them to France. Only that time she had just been telling off one grown-up. Now she was telling off a whole room of them. "All you ever talk about is Kosovo, Kosovo, Kosovo. You

154

keep saying Jasmina has to stop being Albanian if she becomes a Christian. *Why*? Why can't she be both? You want to live in this tiny little world of Albanians all the time, and all the Albanians in that tiny little world have to be the same. But guess what? We're not *in* Kosovo. We're in England. In England, they let us live here and get British passports and still be Muslim, even though they're Christians—or they say they are. We're not very Muslim just like they aren't very Christian, and yet you're making this big fuss because Jasmina, who probably knows more about the Qur'an than any of us, has decided to believe in a different holy book. And you're going to tell her that she can't be Albanian and she can't be from Kosovo and she can't be part of this family and she can't be part of your tiny little world unless she thinks exactly like you! You're all—" she stopped, remembering the argument she had had with Sophie that spring. Then she said, "You're all a bunch of bigots!"

Zari stopped. Everyone was still staring at her. She realised then that she had not only told off all the grown-ups, but she had done it in *shqip*, and she hadn't made any mistakes. "By the way," she added, "I don't think I'll be taking *shqip* lessons any more."

Boba said, "Zari, go to your room."

"Why?" asked Zari. "I'm right. Come on, Boba, you know I'm right."

"Zari," said Boba, more firmly, "go to your room."

Zari went to her room.

# Trees

*N*oneh hardly spoke to Zari at all for a week after that evening. She was upset because Zahe had been upset and told her she was never going to visit her again and what kind of woman allowed her girls to grow up to be so rude to their elders? Zari felt sorry for Noneh, but only a little bit. "Now Anita can come over again," she said once, to Noneh's back, while Noneh was cooking and still not speaking to her. "She's hardly been here at all for months—ever since you started on that wedding stuff—and she was always much nicer than Zahe. You didn't have to try to make her like you."

Noneh didn't say anything, but the next day when Zari came home from school, Anita was sitting on the settee with Noneh watching Albanian videos. Ahmed was playing with some of his toys on the floor. Zari thought he looked much bigger than when she had seen him last. She thought he might be a little bit more fun to play with now that he could talk, but she had other things to do. "Hiya, Anita! Hiya, Ahmed!" she called, as she went up the stairs.

Jasmina was in the bedroom putting her clothes into a suitcase. Boba had bought her the suitcase in the High Street that morning. It wasn't very big, but Jasmina didn't have very many things to put in it, so that was all right. "Hiya, Jasmina," Zari said, slapping her school-bag down on her bed and then flopping herself down next to it. "All right?"

"Yes," said Jasmina, looking a little surprised in spite of herself. "I went to the Job Centre to see about jobs, and Dina said as long as I'm looking, I can stay with her for free until I find one. Of course once I do find one, I'll try to make up the rent. I looked at her flat, and she's got a whole extra room I can stay in; her other flatmate moved out last month, and she was looking for someone to share with again. It's just too perfect—I can't believe it!"

"What did Boba and Noneh say?" Zari asked.

"After all that yelling the last few days," Jasmina chuckled, "Noneh burst into tears and said, 'I can't believe my Jasmina is moving away'!"

"And Boba?"

"Boba didn't say anything. I don't know—he's been

looking upset for a while, but I can't quite tell why. I don't know if he's upset about my decision or about my moving or...about something else. But he did buy me the suitcase. And take me to the Job Centre. And he listened to you that night. True, I don't get to stay and be treated like part of the family, but at least I'm not locked up for the rest of my life. At least I get to live again, and make my own decisions. But what about you, Zari? What do you think?"

"I wish you didn't do it, Jasmina," said Zari. "I wish it was all like before. I wish I could still visit Mrs Jamaica and you could still live here and Noneh wasn't upset again all the time and Boba was smiling like usual and Agron wasn't in trouble and Ekrem was teasing me at school. I wish you were going to marry Sokol—only I'm sort of glad I don't have to take *shqip* lessons from Zahe any more. But you have to make your own decision, Jasmina. That's what they tell us in school—we have to be our own people and do what we think is right, so if you really think this is right, then you have to do it."

"What do *you* think is right, Zari?" Jasmina asked. "You know about Jesus. Don't you want to follow him, too?"

Zari was quiet for what seemed like a very long time. The question made her feel as if she had known something once and forgotten it, and needed desperately to remember it, or do it, or tell it to someone, or something, but that didn't make any sense. She just needed to answer Jasmina's question. She thought about Jesus and thought he might have done all the things they said he did—He must have done, in fact, because they said it in school, and besides, Mrs Jamaica had said it, and she didn't lie—except for that one time, and then she had admitted to it. She thought Jesus must be a very wonderful person, but Jasmina was also a very wonderful person and Zari was—well, just Zari, and maybe Jesus wouldn't notice her anyhow.

Then she thought about Noneh and how tired she looked all the time, and that if she became a Christian, Noneh would probably become so upset she would get sick. It had happened once before, when Boba had left them all in Kosovo years ago. Zari didn't remember that time, but Jasmina and Agron had told her about it. She thought about Boba, and how whatever he was angry about would probably overflow and explode if another of his daughters decided to stop being a Muslim. She knew Jasmina was lucky, and if they had had a different sort of Boba, much worse things could have happened to her—worse even than being locked up in her room for the rest of her life. Being a Christian, Zari thought, was probably a good idea, only it was too hard. When Mrs Jamaica had become one, her whole family had gotten angry, too, and they weren't even from a different religion. Christians said that following Jesus was the only way to get to know God and go to Paradise, but Zari thought there must be other ways, too. Surely if she was good enough, God would let her in. It wasn't like she was a really important person or anything.

All of a sudden she noticed she had been thinking aloud. She wondered how much of her thoughts she had spoken. She saw Jasmina looking at her very hard. Zari blushed. "Maybe I'll do it when I'm older," she said. "But look, Jasmina, I'm too young. It's not like I can move out if Noneh and Boba get angry at me."

"Maybe Dina would say you could stay with us. I could look after you."

Zari looked at her sister sceptically. "That would never work," she said. "You're too busy anyway. And I would have to change to a different school, when I finally have real friends at this one."

But the next day Zari didn't go to school when Sajda knocked for her in the morning. Boba said he'd take her to help Jasmina move into Dina's flat. Zari was sure this was the only time anyone in her family would ever take her to see Jasmina again—at least for a very long time— so she wanted to make certain she got there this once.

Jasmina got into the front seat, and Zari sat in the back with the things that didn't fit into the car boot. Jasmina had said she didn't have very much, but it seemed like a whole pile of new things had appeared from somewhere overnight. Zari knew Anita had brought some things, and she was pretty sure Boba had bought a few presents along with the suitcase. Included among the gifts was a nice new set of tea glasses, like the ones they drank out of as a family. Jasmina had cried when she saw them. "Who will drink tea out of these with me?" she asked. "You'll have to come visit." No one had answered.

Now Noneh stood in the doorway, with her arms folded tightly in front of her. She looked as if she wanted to cry, too, but she wasn't doing it. Her face was tight and Zari thought she would need some comforting when she got back. Boba pulled the car away from the pavement and they set off for Jasmina's new home.

There was a block of flats right behind the tube station. Dina's flat was on the fourth floor. Jasmina loaded up her arms with the box of tea glasses and some other kitchen things, Boba carried the suitcase and a lamp, and Zari followed both of them with her own arms full of bathroom towels. They got into the lift and Boba pushed the button with the number four on it.

Dina was home. She looked like she was about Jasmina's age, and Jasmina's height as well, but her accent when she spoke English was Italian instead of Albanian. She seemed very happy to see all of them. She led them all into her sitting room and made them sit down and drink tea. She made tea in mugs like the English, and she put milk in it, too, just like they did. "I started drinking it this way in the English classes," she confessed, "and I actually like it now."

"We drink tea like this at home, too," Zari said. "In the afternoons, when we aren't usually drinking Albanian tea."

Boba and Jasmina remained completely silent, and Zari started to feel embarrassed for having spoken, but Dina smiled at her and passed her the sugar. Zari put five spoonfuls of sugar in her mug, and Dina didn't even look surprised.

Boba finished drinking his tea in about three gulps, which amazed Zari, because it had been very hot. He sat there looking as though he would rather be somewhere else, and so finally Jasmina whispered something to Dina and Dina said to Boba, "Would you like to start settling Jasmina's things into her room? You know which one it is." Boba got up without a word, taking the lamp and the suitcase with him, and disappeared down the hallway.

After that, Dina asked Zari all kinds of questions about herself, and Jasmina smiled, and sometimes teased her quietly. Zari wondered what Jasmina and Dina would talk about once she and Boba left. She supposed that, since the two of them were friends, they might have already talked about everything, and that would be boring. But then she remembered that she and her friends never seemed to run out of anything to talk about. There just seemed to be more and more things the longer they were friends. Maybe it would be like that for Jasmina, too. Zari hoped so. She wanted her sister to be happy.

They didn't stay very long in the end. Boba waited in the hallway outside the lift while Jasmina gave Zari a long hug goodbye. Zari didn't want to think that maybe this would be the last time she would see her sister. She decided then and there that when she was old enough to go places by herself like Agron, she would walk to Jasmina's every week to drink tea with her out of those tea glasses.

Boba didn't say anything in the car all the way home, and Zari didn't say anything either. She realised that she was still a little bit angry at her parents. How could they make Jasmina leave? She pressed her face against the car window. Usually Boba told her off for this, because it always left a mark on the glass, but this time he didn't mention it.

They passed rows and rows of trees growing out of the tiny dirt squares which interrupted the pavement. The trees had dropped more of their leaves, Zari noticed. She could see that the branch stubs had all sprouted tiny little twigs, which is what the leaves were dropping off of now. They were clever, those trees. They found a way to grow and be pretty and green no matter what happened to them. But next spring, they'd all be cut again. It wasn't fair. They reminded Zari of Jasmina. Jasmina was a refugee twice. First the Serbs made her leave Kosovo with the family, and now the family had made her leave them. That wasn't fair either.

Boba parked the car in front of the house. He let Zari out on the pavement but stayed in the car himself. He was going to work, even though he was late. "Don't go to school today," he told her as she clambered out of the car. "Your mother will need you."

He was right. Noneh was still in her dressing gown, and she looked terrible. Zari supposed she had probably looked terrible at breakfast time, too, only she hadn't noticed it then. Noneh's face looked rather grey, and there were great dark shadows under her eyes. "Can I make you some tea, Noneh?" Noneh nodded, and went into the sitting room and lay down on the settee. She wrapped herself up in a big blanket she had taken off her bed upstairs. Zari made the tea—English tea, because it was still morning, and brought it to her with some biscuits.

"It will be all right, Noneh," Zari said, as they sipped their tea together. "She was grown up anyway. It's good for her to live somewhere else. And we can always go visit her. She doesn't live so far away. I'll go with you. You'd like to see her flat."

"She's a Christian," Noneh whispered. "Christian" still sounded like a swear word when Noneh said it.

"But she's your daughter," said Zari. "Just like me. And we both love you."

Noneh burst into tears. "You're not going to be a Christian, too, are you?" she asked when she had stopped sobbing a bit.

Zari tried hard not to think about Jesus or Jasmina. "No," she said, while she wasn't thinking about them.

But when she went upstairs later, after Noneh had fallen asleep, she found a card on her bed. It looked like it had been hand-drawn, and Zari remembered that once Jasmina had told her that one of her college friends was an artist. Zari guessed he must have drawn it. It was a picture of Jesus on the cross, but He didn't look sad and helpless like he did in so many similar pictures. He looked as if, at any moment, he'd come back to life, jump off that cross, and change the world. On the back, Jasmina had written, "You <u>are</u> important. This is why."

Zari looked at the picture for a very long time. She started to get sleepy, and the sleepiness made her think of crosses, and the crosses started to look like trees— chopped off, stumpy trees, but trees all the same. She imagined the cross-tree growing leaves, just like the trees growing out of the pavement in her street. The leaves grew and grew in her mind, from twigs. The twigs grew into branches, and the branches grew up and up, and out and out, until they stretched over the houses. People came to try to cut down those branches, as well. They thought they were big and dark and in the way. Zari thought they thought that about refugees, too. Sometimes the branches fell when the people cut them, but they always grew back, and soon they were shading all of London—not with darkness, but with peace.

When she woke up, it was still early afternoon. She tiptoed into her parents bedroom at the front of the house to make sure she had only dreamed about the cross-tree. She had, which was a shame, because if it had been real she could probably have climbed the branch that was touching her window in the dream, down to the trunk where Jesus was, and if she climbed from there along another one, she would end up all the way at Jasmina's flat. This would be convenient because then she could go visit Jasmina whenever she wanted, and Noneh and Boba would probably never know. Then she had a better idea.

She tiptoed back out of her parents' room and down the stairs. Noneh was still lying on the couch, but she wasn't asleep. "Noneh," said Zari, "can Jasmina give me *shqip* lessons now? She still speaks good *shqip*, doesn't she? I know, it's not as perfect as Zahe's but we didn't speak perfect *shqip* in Kosovo when we lived there anyway, did we? And she can read it and write it, still. And I don't want to forget it all."

Noneh looked at her and smiled for the first time in days. "You're the clever one, Zari. Always the clever one. I will talk about it with your father."

Zari smiled, too. Maybe things would get better after all. It might be quite nice to have a sister living in her own flat if she could still visit her. It would make Zari feel grown up, too. It would give her something to talk to Sajda and Gemma about. They would be jealous.

Suddenly there was a knock at the door. Noneh looked a little embarrassed, because she had done nothing to her hair or clothes all day. But she shrugged and got up. Zari crept up behind her to see who it was. The shape they could see through the textured glass in the door looked like Mrs Jamaica's shape. Zari saw Noneh hesitate. None of them had talked to Mrs Jamaica since Jasmina had made her announcement weeks ago. Then Noneh reached forward and opened the door.

It *was* Mrs Jamaica. She stood there with a plate in her hands. There was a cake on it. "I baked too many of these today," she said. "I thought your family might like it."

Noneh looked at the cake. She looked at Mrs Jamaica. Then she said, "Come in, Mrs Dix."

Zari had forgotten Mrs Jamaica's name was really Mrs Dix, and she almost forgot it was also Mrs Jamaica, because she was so surprised that Noneh had invited her in.

"Thank you for cake," Noneh was saying in English. She took it and went with it to the kitchen.

Zari led Mrs Jamaica into the sitting room. They both sat down in different chairs and looked at each other. Mrs Jamaica looked almost as surprised as Zari felt, and even a little uncomfortable. Finally she said quietly, "I never expected to be invited in. I thought I'd just leave the cake, if I were lucky."

"It means it will get better, Mrs Jamaica," Zari said. "She wouldn't have let you in if it wasn't going to get better."

In a few minutes, Noneh came back with a tray. There were biscuits on it, but no cake. Their family didn't offer their guests something that the guest had brought as a gift. There was also tea. But it wasn't English tea—it was Albanian, even though it was still afternoon. "You try Albanian tea?" Noneh asked Mrs Jamaica.

"I would *love* to try your tea," answered Mrs Jamaica.

Zari heard voices outside, and jumped up as Noneh was pouring the tea, so she could open the door before Sajda or Gemma knocked.

"Sajda! Gemma!" she cried. "Come in! Noneh's serving Albanian tea! You have to try some."

The three girls stepped into the living room, and Sajda and Gemma both whispered, "What's *she* doing here?" in surprise when they saw Mrs Jamaica.

"She just came," Zari whispered back. "And Noneh actually let her in."

"You try Albanian tea?" Noneh asked the girls, with a faint smile on her face.

"Yes, please," they said, a little shyly. The afternoon had suddenly become strange. They always played together outdoors; they had almost never been inside each other's houses. Now here they were at Zari's house, and her mother was offering them Albanian tea.

"It's very good," they told her.

"It's delicious," said Mrs Jamaica. "I've heard so much about this tea."

Noneh only smiled. But Zari smiled bigger. It wasn't that things were going to get better. It was that they were already getting better. Here they were, she and her mother, two Kosovars, drinking tea with a Briton, a

Pakistani, and a Jamaican. This was how it was supposed to be. She knew that now. She wished she knew a Serbian girl, so she could have invited her, too. "Tomorrow," she said, "let's do this at Jasmina's."

Noneh stopped smiling, but she didn't say no. "We'll see," she said instead. "We'll see."

When Zari let their visitors out a little later so they could all go home, she looked very hard at the trees. It was autumn, and the leaves were falling, and the trees shouldn't have been growing at this time of year at all, but she could have sworn she saw more branches on them than had been there in the morning.

# Glossary

When Zari moved to London, she had to learn English—a whole new language. But sometimes, even people who speak the same language have different meanings for certain words. Below are some words from the story which have a different meaning in Zari's London than they do in the United States. They are followed by the words or meanings many North Americans would use instead.

*Biscuits* – Cookies

*Block of Flats* – Apartment building

*Car boot* – Trunk of a car

*Chips* – French fries

*Council House* – Government-owned, welfare housing

*College* – Junior college

*Cooker* – Stove

*Flatmate* – Roommate

*Football* – Soccer (A *footballer* is a football/soccer player.)

*Hiya!* – Hi! Hello!

*Holiday* – Vacation

*Infants' School* – The very lowest grades of elementary school. (Zari would have called elementary school, "Primary School.")

*Lorry* – Trailer truck

*Maths* – Math
*Over the Road* – Across the street
*Packet of Crisps* – Bag of chips
*Pavement* – Sidewalk
*R.E.* – Religious Education class
*Reception Year* – Kindergarten
*Revise for Exams* – Study for exams
*Rows* – Arguments
*Science Investigation* – Science experiment
*Settee* – Couch, sofa
*Summer Holidays* – Summer vacation
*Terraced Houses* – Row houses
*To Fancy Someone* – To have a crush on someone
*Torches* – Flashlights
*Train Carriage* – The car of a train
*Tube Station* – Subway station
*Windscreen* – Windshield

# Author's Page

*E*ven when she was a girl, Jennifer Anne Grosser loved to travel and get to know people from other countries. She also loves introducing her friends to Jesus. In her early twenties, she moved to London, England, to work with refugees in the East End. Five years later, she moved to the United States again, where she lives in a pretty house surrounded by trees which are not growing out of the pavement, and wishes she had a dog. Besides writing and spending time with friends, she works in a coffee shop getting to know the people of Worcester, Massachusetts, and trying to love Jesus better and better. *Trees in the Pavement* is her first book.

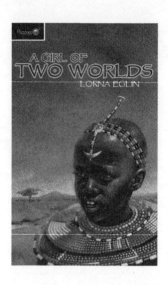

A GIRL OF TWO WORLDS
BY LORNA EGLIN

Nosim is proud to be Maasai and to be the first member of
her tribe to go to school. But can she follow the old ways of
the Maasai tribe and be a modern, educated young woman?
Can she still belong to her family and belong to the Jesus
Christ she hears to much about at school?

ISBN: 978-1-85792-839-6

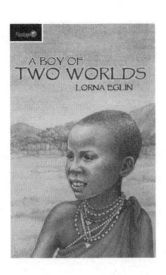

A BOY OF TWO WORLDS
BY LORNA EGLIN

Lemayan, a boy from the Maasai tribe in East Africa is a
gifted goat herder. But one day a drought attacks their
pasture and their whole way of life is affected. Worms
infect the cattle and they have to sell them. To make things
worse, Lemayan falls sick. In this story Lemayan finds out
that a good shepherd cares for his sheep and that Jesus
cares for him.

ISBN: 978-1-84550-126-6

CHRISTIAN FOCUS PUBLICATIONS

Christian Focus | Christian Heritage | CF4K | Mentor

Christian Focus Publications publishes books for adults and children under its four main imprints: Christian Focus, CF4K, Mentor and Christian Heritage. Our books reflect that God's word is reliable and Jesus is the way to know him, and live for ever with him.

Our children's publication list includes a Sunday School curriculum that covers pre-school to early teens; puzzle and activity books. We also publish personal and family devotional titles, biographies and inspirational stories that children will love.

If you are looking for quality Bible teaching for children then we have an excellent range of Bible story and age specific theological books.

From pre-school to teenage fiction, we have it covered!

**Find us at our web page:
www.christianfocus.com**

**CF4•K**
*Because you're never
too young to know Jesus*